Awesome Wonder
The Gift of Remembrance

M. Ann Ricks

PublishAmerica
Baltimore

First printing

ISBN: 1-4241-8487-8
PUBLISHED BY PUBLISHAMERICA, LLLP
www.publishamerica.com
Baltimore

Printed in the United States of America

"But the Comforter, which is the Holy Ghost, whom the Father will send in my name, he shall teach you all things, and bring all things to your remembrance, whatsoever I have said unto you."—John 14:26

Chapter 1

The discussion last night continued to leave me unsettled. Although a lot of what was said was true, the question remained: why did I continue to feel like something was missing?

As I lay in bed, I closed my eyes and began to take stock of my life. I have a wonderful and loving husband who is very easy on the eyes. A son whom both my husband and I are very proud of and a career that is paying the bills. I love my house and the neighborhood. We are not debt-free but we are on the right road, thanks to my husband and we are all in good health. So what else is there?

Every day I was haunted with a feeling of loss. Was loss the right word? It's as if there was a void in my life that desperately needed to be filled. My mind constantly searched for what could be missing but always came up empty.

As done on every other day, I decided to eventually go about my day as those thoughts temporarily faded into the background only to re-emerge as a constant reminder that my life was missing something or even someone.

It was an overcast Monday morning, the worst kind of morning, especially if you are already feeling like crap about life. My husband was snoring and I was next to him, wide awake at 5:30a.m. It was too early to get up but I couldn't continue to stay there knowing that I could be doing something productive. I moved to exit the bed as gingerly as possible but Justin moved toward me to encircle me into his arms. He must have radar.

"Where ya going, babe?" he slurred, eyes still closed.

"Nowhere. Go back to sleep," I said softly and kissed his ear. Thankfully, he rolled over and resumed the "calling of the hogs." I walked over to the window, sat down on the mauve cushioned window seat and looked out at the day. *Do I really want to face this day?* I asked inwardly and sighed as I took in the grayness of my view and watched the clouds slowly move across the sky. "Do I have a choice?" I responded to myself aloud, knowing that talking back to oneself is not good. I chuckled. As if on cue, my mind pressed "play" and I walked back across the bedroom into my bathroom. I looked at myself in the mirror. Almond-colored eyes looked back at me strangely expectant. My skin, the color of caramel, was thankfully, clear and youthful. The full lips that used to cause me so much emotional pain as a child are now my proudest asset. I pulled my shoulder-length dark brown hair back into a pubescent ponytail and covered it with a shower cap. Loni, my older sister, would always laugh and tell her friends that I was the only black person that she knew who put their hair in a ponytail to bathe. Because I was and am a movie junkie, I thought that it was what you did. Apparently, I was wrong but I never stopped and it became a ritual.

The water ran down onto the floor of the shower stall and I found myself just staring as it gathered and then escaped down the drain. I don't know how long I stood there naked. The water hypnotized me. I was standing at the opening of the shower door wondering if I could escape life as easily as the water traveled down the drain. Would I come back as a new pellet of water? I shook my head to refocus, knowing that there was no way I could escape life at this juncture. I didn't really want to escape. As I tried to direct my thoughts elsewhere, I heard running water in the bathroom adjacent to mine. It was Adam, my son. My baby boy. I felt a smile begin to take dominion over my countenance as I entered the shower. No pellets for me.

The water and suds felt good but it only succeeded in cleansing my body, not my mind. I was hoping that I would have a clearer, not to

6

mention cleaner, perspective once I finished my shower. That was not be, unfortunately.

As I toweled off and began to moisturize with Shea butter, a faint knock on the already open door caught my attention. Adam was standing at the bathroom entrance rubbing his eyes with his coffee-colored fists.

"Mommy?" Adam breathed, "you are up early again."

I opened my arms and he instinctively walked into the bathroom and hugged me. He stepped back and considered me standing before him in my pink bra and panties with a question in his eyes. "Why do you love pink so much?"

I smiled and asked, "Why do you love Scooby-Doo so much?"

He shrugged and I mimicked his action. We smiled at each other and a faint giggle escaped his perfect mouth. I then asked with a touch of concern, "Did you have an accident?"

"No, I just wanted to see what you were doin'," he mumbled, as he looked down at the dusty rose and white tiled floor.

"Mommy couldn't sleep so she is starting her day. Is that okay with you?"

In the back of my mind, I wondered why I spoke in the third person when conversing with him.

"Yes, Mommy. It's okay. Can I go back to sleep?" he responded, and turned to look at his father sprawled across the bed making night noises. He giggled and scrunched up his face as only a child could do.

"Come on. I'll walk with you to your room," I offered, extending my hand.

We held hands and walked to his room. Being a seven-year-old and tall for his age, he was too big for me to carry, even piggyback. He climbed into bed and closed his eyes. I covered him in with his Scooby-Doo comforter and just stared at him. He was so perfectly brown and smooth. I could easily visualize what Justin looked like as a boy when I looked into Adam's face. As he turned his head to get in a comfortable position, I kissed his forehead.

"Sweet dreams, baby," I said, knowing that I'd have to wake him in a couple of hours.

Walking past Adam's bathroom, I noticed that the toilet seat was up and wondered if the male species was born not knowing how to place the toilet seat down. Was it some kind of physical handicap or what? It never ends. The little lift to my sullen mood was over. I audibly sighed, placed the seat down, grabbed the clothes hamper and headed down the stairs to the laundry room.

As I separated the clothes, my mind took me back to my childhood. Every morning my mother rose early and the first order of business was to bring the dirty clothes from the hampers down to the laundry room to wash clothes. It is funny how we adults continue our parents' traditions and habits and are oblivious to the fact that we are just continuing the saga.

Just thinking about my mom made me want to call her and talk to her about the way I had been feeling. The emptiness and overwhelming inner dissatisfaction were weighing on me. Although the first person that I should be sharing this with should be my husband, sometimes men, as wonderful as they are, would think that it was either something that they were not doing or something that had to be easily remedied. Some suggested a new project or money. I honestly didn't think that there was anything that Justin could say or do to help. Needless to say, I didn't want him to worry about me and I didn't want to burden him.

I decided that I would call Mom once Adam was off at day camp and Justin was at work. Before I started my workday, I'd have a heart-to-heart with her.

After exiting the laundry room I closed the door because I didn't want to wake anyone with the sound of the washer, I turned and saw Justin standing in the kitchen as if he was waiting for me.

The kitchen was more length than width and he was standing in front of the refrigerator at the far end, acting as if he were looking for something inside. I glanced at the clock on the range and noticed that it was 6:45a.m.

"Hey," I said with a smile as I kissed him good-morning. I could taste toothpaste and smell that he had already taken a shower. I always liked the way he smelled. Regardless of what cologne he wore, I could always smell his scent underneath. I could only describe it as "soapy." His fragrance was fresh and clean.

"Hey, Mommy," he returned as his arms encircled my waist. "You still not sleeping? What is on your mind? When you are sleeping, you are tossing. A few nights ago, you looked like you were running." He looked at me with a smile on his full lips but I could see the concern in his chocolate eyes. His hair was freshly trimmed and his beard looked so neat and perfect, he could have been one of those models in the hair magazines. Looking at him made me think of the conversation that served as a revelation about my life.

"I am okay. Work stuff…. Sometimes I feel like it is not what I should be doing."

Giving him another peck on his lips, I retreated from his embrace. Oddly enough, sometimes I thought that he could feel my emotions. I didn't want to get into this with him. I would figure out my issue on my own and resolve it. He seemed to sense that I was becoming defensive so I turned away from him and said, "I'll get Adam to camp this morning." Once I was certain that my emotions were in check, I faced him again, giving him my best smile. "What can I make you for breakfast?" I offered, trying to change the subject.

"Paige."

"What's up, baby?"

"We can't always run from this conversation," he stated and retrieved the coffee from the cabinet. "You have to admit that we were making some headway last night until you decided to shut down."

I reluctantly recalled that the dialogue was getting a bit too intrusive. I, obviously not the mature one, caught an unwarranted attitude so we tabled the discussion.

"Baby, I am just a little overworked and tired. Please don't worry."

"I haven't seen you genuinely happy for what seems like forever. You know what they say…if Mommy is not happy…" He let his sentence it trail off.

Summing up all of my manufactured sultriness, I whispered, "So why don't you make Mommy happy?"

Justin's eyes lit up and he started tipping like a pimp in my direction. I laughed at how funny he could be and started running into the family room. I allowed him to catch me; anything to derail the conversation that we were about to have. Talking about it didn't seem to solve anything. I looked at him deeply and saw the love he had for me and the need to protect me in his eyes. "Paige, you know I love you, right?" I nodded, knowing that he did. I also asked myself why that wasn't enough. I realized that sex didn't cure everything but right now I just needed to show my husband that he hadn't anything to worry about. I knew as I allowed him to kiss my neck and slowly remove my robe that I was being deceptive. He opened my robe and eventually unfastened the bra revealing my breasts. Making love to avoid a conversation that would have made me feel worse was far better than starting off this day with an argument. As he gave me all of his love, I knew that a part of me needed him and all that he wanted to give. I whispered my satisfaction. We enjoyed each other until he couldn't hold back his culmination. I smiled. He was going to have a good day.

Chapter 2

"Mom, it's like I am not really living. I don't know if I can put my finger on it but something is not right. My life is not complete."

"Paige, it seems like this is something that has been going on for a long time. Are you spending time with yourself? You know that we sometimes get lost in our family's lives and forget that we are important," Mom said.

It was clear that she wanted to say something else but was hesitant.

"Justin tries to let me have my time. I don't really have any girlfriends in my area and all of my acquaintances are through Adam's activities. People at work can't be totally trusted save maybe two but I don't think that my lack of time to myself is the cause."

I felt the entrance of frustration and didn't want it to take up residence in our conversation.

"Paige, I know you don't want to hear this but, I think that you need to pray about this."

Okay, here she goes, I thought. She knew that I haven't put stock in God in sometime. My childhood and teen years were filled with Sunday school, Youth Group, etc. My sisters and I were in the midst of any and every activity that was remotely connected with the church and Jesus. I had a great deal of resentment and it stemmed from what I saw when

I was a child through young adulthood. The church, or at least *my* church, was filled with a cast of characters and when I realized the truth about the people that I looked up to, my relationship with Jesus was irrevocably altered.

"Mom," I said, sounding exasperated.

"I know you have your issues, but you need to get past them and know that the people that you have issues with are human. All have sinned, Paige. I have always told you that you can't put your trust in man."

She paused and I heard a muffled voice in the background. It sounded like my dad. I realized that I had better put and end to this call before she asked if I wanted to speak to him. I didn't want to lie but also didn't want to have what I would consider an insincere conversation with him.

"I'll think about what you are saying, Mom. Understand that I am not mad at God, I know who He is."

"I know. I love you and I am and praying for you," she said. I could visualize her wearing the smile that she always wore when she was certain that she knew better than anyone else.

Harden not your heart...

I paused a moment, unsure if my mother had said what I thought I heard. I decided not to ask her to repeat it.

"I love you too, Mom. Tell Dad I said hi. I gotta to get back to work."

Disappointed that Mom and I weren't able to talk like I wanted, I walked to the kitchen and obtained a glass, filled it with ice and then water. I like to crunch on the ice. The goal was to try and trick my mind into thinking that I was actually eating something so I wouldn't grab a cookie. Sometimes it worked, sometimes it didn't.

I actually dreaded checking my e-mails but knew that I had to start my day. My profession, an account representative for an insurance company, could be rewarding at times. Unfortunately, healthcare costs were increasing and the government was doing absolutely nothing about it. The more the rates increased, the more I had to figure out ways to strategize with our clients to make benefit design changes. That strategy ultimately required shifting the costs to the actual employee. We tried not to communicate this plan outright but essentially this is what the end result had been and has to be. This couldn't go on forever but it was my job.

My employer, BetterHealthNet, Inc., or BHN, one of the larger players in the industry, tried to remain competitive. To do that, they joined the rest of the healthcare carriers and introduced new products that promote consumer accountability. This would unfortunately not eliminate the need to raise costs across the board. It certainly would not alleviate the problem facing the nation but it provided a new spin which emphasized making the employee more accountable. The idea was selling. Who knew for how long? Many people had not received cost of living increases but continued to have to endure the cost of healthcare increasing year after year with prescription costs being the catalyst. It was really not easy to meet with our membership to deliver a message that, although cost-effective, did not solve the problem. Thankfully, I minored in performing arts.

On the positive side, being able to work from home was absolutely wonderful. I have learned to multi-task more efficiently for home and work. Although I was aligned to work in a segment of my company that is somewhat unorthodox, I tried to make the best of the situation. What makes it tolerable was that I didn't work in the actual office. Thankfully most of my account teams shared the same service philosophy. We all had the same "field service work mentality" or so we are told because of our history in the industry. We strive to be honest with our clients and do our best keep them satisfied from a service perspective. I have to say that I have worked quite cohesively with my colleagues except for one team, the Rosenfeld account team.

An e-mail with a red flag popped in and grabbed my attention. It was from one of my client contacts. It stated that a member was in need of some assistance with regard to an unpaid claim. It was denied because the member was showing as terminated and as result hadn't any medical coverage. This was a typical member eligibility issue. I really hated claims issues but because this could easily snowball into a screwy eligibility matter, I provided assistance. At least this group appreciated the work

I did for them. I immediately sent the eligibility analyst assigned to this account an e-mail requesting confirmation of the member's eligibility to get the ball rolling and copied in the claims person so that they could reprocess the claim and any other claims that had been denied in error. The one claim brought to my attention may not have been the only one that was denied erroneously. The team assigned to service this account, NY Solutions, was a good one. Once eligibility has remedied the error, the claim would be forwarded for processing. I'd respond back to the client and close it out.

A few more issues came across that required my assistance and much to my dismay, I had to sit in on a couple of thirty-minute conference calls to discuss nothing.

I resolved the issues and decided that I needed to step away from the desk for a breather. I glanced at the clock at the bottom right hand of my computer and realized that it was close to 1:30 p.m. My morning had flown by and I still had some client communications projects to get started on. I decided that they could wait and stood to my feet. Standing up on my toes and having a good stretch felt good. While wiggling my fingers in the air, my stomach growled. Lunch was calling. Descending the stairs, I heard my home phone ringing. I grunted and although apprehensive, decided that I'd better see who was calling.

Looking at the caller ID, I recognized my sister Loni's telephone number.

Against my better judgment, I answered the phone.

"Hi, Loni."

"Oh, you knew it was me?"

"Yeah, silly. Caller ID!?" I rolled my eyes.

"How are you?" she asked. She sounded unusually cheerful and I wondered what was next.

"I am good. You okay?" Bracing myself, I switched ears and placed the phone on my shoulder.

"I am great! I got a job offer and it is in Texas!" She sounded as if she were bursting at the seams. I could just picture her with a big Kool-Aid grin on her face.

"Loni, that is great!" I was truly happy for her. She seemed to have to announce all career wins. I was always very excited for her but in the back of my mind, I wondered what kind of response she wanted when she shared her news. In previous instances, she became crestfallen when I congratulated her. Did I say something wrong? Loni was a mystery. For some crazy reason, she felt as though she didn't measure up. She had a bachelor of science degree and had completed pharmacy school at the top of her class. She knew more about medicines and treatments than anyone I knew. Because she had work experience in her field and the appropriate education, she was making a very good living.

"Paige, this will mean that I may have to move to Dallas."

Here it comes, I thought to myself.

"Do you think that you'll be okay with living so far from home?" I knew that she would become homesick but would unsuccessfully try and fake the funk until it became unbearable. "Tyler may not be ready to pick up and move to Dallas," I reminded her.

Tyler, Loni's husband, had his own internet business. He created and sold website designs. He could actually work anywhere but would he want to?

"Yeah." The first signs of uncertainty audibly surfaced.

"You sure? Couldn't you have found anything closer? Why so far? I don't know what you are running from but whatever it is, you can't keep running from it because it's a part of you."

Loni had a track record for obtaining positions in remote parts of the country to prove her independence but she always found a reason to leave the job to return home. This was her M.O. until she met and married Tyler a year ago. I didn't realize that I was interrogating her like a cross-examining prosecutor until I heard sniffles. I immediately felt ashamed. Why did she have to be so touchy?

"Why can't you be happy for me? This is a good opportunity."

"I am happy for you. I do hope that you are taking this job for the right reasons," I stated rationally.

"And what, Oprah…what would be the right reasons?" she said beginning to own a defensive tone.

"You have tried this before and what happened?"

"You sound just like Celia." Knowing that Celia (my other sister) and I are usually on the same page, I felt vindicated.

15

"Are we both wrong?" I asked, growing weary from this conversation. *What are you running from, Paige? I am a part of you too.* I know Loni didn't say that. I was shaken for a few seconds then decided to let the call take another course.

"Loni, be excited, but be careful. I wish you success. If you decide to take it, we'll all be out to see you and Tyler."

That should do it, I thought, hoping that it would end this part of the conversation.

"I haven't decided to take it and of course I have to talk this over with Tyler, but thanks."

We continued to chat about a few minor familial issues like what my family is doing for the rest of the summer and how Adam was doing. Blah, blah, blah. I reiterated my happiness for her and hoped that she would make the best decision for herself and her family. Finally, the call ended and I made my way back downstairs into the kitchen to get something to eat. It was about 2:15 p.m. and I was really hungry. I arrived at the decision to have a honey ham and cheese sandwich with chips. Quick and easy.

The rest of the afternoon was a blur and I found myself getting ready to pick up Adam from camp. My mind rewound itself to my conversation with Loni. *Am I running from something?* I didn't think that I was but I was sure as heck not running *to* anything.

That was the second time that I heard something or someone. What was my problem?

Chapter 3

Lost in thought while placing clothes in my closet, I failed to hear my office phone ringing until I heard the voice of my best friend, Karlie, coming through. I ran from the back of my walk-in closet to my office down the hall and pressed the speaker button.

"Hey there," I said, out of breath.

"How dare you screen your calls?" she snapped, feigning an attitude.

"Girl, I am done for the day and you know I don't answer this phone after 5:00 p.m."

"Sorry. I just had to call you and ask if you were okay. It was just placed on my heart to call you. You know I have to follow my heart."

"Don't tell me, Karlie, the Spirit convicted you to call me." I rolled my eyes.

Karlie is my best friend in the world but she is saved. I am mean *really* saved. She's no joke. She speaks to the Lord like He is actually a physical human being. She actually has a relationship with her Jesus. Her confidence in Him was wonderful to witness but I was not feelin' it. She accepted Christ when she was a teenager but backslid in her twenties (her words, not mine), and recommitted herself about five years ago. Now, watch out!

"Don't hate, celebrate!" she said with a chuckle. "I just wanted to touch base with you because I had a feeling that you were and have been out of sorts for sometime. Don't try to fool me, Paige, 'cause I've known you too many years. I haven't heard from you in about two weeks and that is two weeks too long."

"I am fine," I lied.

"What did I say?" she countered, sounding like someone's mother. Well, she was someone's mother, just not mine.

"I'm just a little out of sorts."

"What does that mean?"

I sucked my teeth, beginning to act like someone's child and confessed. "I don't know what the matter is, I just feel like my life is incomplete. Something is not right and I don't know how to make it right." I paused, not sure how to explain my issue. "I don't think that I'd know where to start if I had a clue as to what the matter was."

"Can I suggest something?" She made this inquiry a little too gingerly. Almost as if she didn't want to say something but felt compelled to.

"Go ahead," I sighed, and then held my breath as if I were about to get hit in the stomach.

"Can we pray about this? I believe that is why I was led to call you."

As much as I wanted to tell her no, I heard myself say yes. After all, I trusted Karlie. I didn't know if I trusted the Lord anymore but it couldn't hurt.

She breathed audibly and began, "Jesus, first of all we thank you for the gift of friendship. We thank you that through You we can feel whole not because of who we are but because of who You are. Lord, we come to You asking for your direction and intervention. We don't know what the problem is, but we ask that because You are wisdom, you can assist and reveal the issue. We trust that You can deliver us from any circumstance, realizing that we are your children and You promised that You would raise up a standard against anything that threatens to harm one of your own. We leave this matter in your hands. Bless her with patience. Lord, we thank You for the victory right now in the matchless name of Jesus as we can do all things through You and only You. Amen."

"Thanks for praying, girl," I said, trying to sound genuine.

"I just thought that before I tried to give any advice, I'd better take it to the Lord first." I could see her smile through the phone. I wished I had her maturity. Was it really maturity? She just believed and just knew that it was going to be alright. She admittedly became flustered and frustrated like the rest of us but she knew that her God could work it out. I envied that but I couldn't see myself trusting or believing in anyone or anything like that anymore.

"Paige? You there?" Karlie asked.

"Yup."

Let's get together so that we can talk face to face. I am coming to visit you. What are you doing Saturday?"

"This Saturday?" I was shocked that she was going to travel to see me. This was unprecedented. She had never done this without planning at least a month in advance.

"Yes, this Saturday."

"Well, nothing. J is taking Adam to a ball game and I was just going to clean the house."

"Well, the house is going to have to wait," she stated with resolve.

"You don't have to tell me twice. I'll see you Saturday." I was excited. "Are you going stay the entire weekend?"

"Yup. I am bringing Tara with me."

"Great!"

"I gotta go, but I'll call you Wednesday to solidify plans."

"I'll see if J can get an extra ticket so that he can take Tara with Adam to the game. It's Triple A so that shouldn't be a problem."

"So let it be written, so let it be done," she said in her Ramaesees imitation. Obviously, too many viewings of *The Ten Commandments*, one of our favorite movies.

I laughed. She was really coming.

"Okay, I'll let you go. I love you, girl."

"Love you too."

My mouth immediately became dry and I couldn't say anything else. What would we unearth this weekend? Maybe we'd find out that I am just peri, peri-menopausal.

Trust in Me. I am here.

There it was again. I knew that I didn't say that.

It always made me smile when I saw Adam and he sprinted towards me screaming, "Mommy, Mommy!" I was surprised anew each time because he was elated to see me.

His teacher, Ms. Debbie, a woman who seemed too old to be a camp counselor, always looked out for him. She reminded me of my mother but of course she was a little younger. She also served as a babysitter whenever Justin and I wanted to get out and do something as a couple.

"Hi there, Ms. Debbie," I greeted.

Adam reached me and gave me the best hug a mother could ever receive.

"Hi, Mrs. Covington," she stated with a warm smile. "He certainly loves his mommy," she observed, nodding down at Adam.

He smiled back at her and proclaimed, "With all of my heart." He planted a kiss on my cheek to prove it.

"Love, you are too much," was my response to his unabashed display of affection. I was so glad that he had not inherited my inhibitions.

"You are blessed, Mrs. Covington," Ms. Debbie offered.

"Thanks," I returned, not knowing how I should respond. "Please, I'd really like you to call me Paige."

"Forgive me, Paige. I just have to get used to calling you by your first name." She smiled and continued. "I can tell that you and your husband are providing the right example of love in your home. So many of the children that I see don't have the proper foundation. Knowing that Jesus is love and the source of love is most important, don't you agree?" She held my gaze as if determined not to let me avert her eyes.

"Love is most important," I confirmed, and quickly turned my attention to Adam.

"Paige, I don't think that I asked you this before but do you know Jesus?" she inquired purposefully but with tenderness lacing her voice.

"I know Jesus but He and I haven't been on speaking terms for some time." I didn't know why I was so honest with Ms. Debbie, but oh, well; it was out there now.

"Is that right?" she said, her head tipped a little to side, obviously surprised by my response. "Well, I know how you can easily remedy that," she stated confidently, with a smile that seemed to be never-ending.

"So I am told," I stated, trying to diplomatically place an end to what I felt bordered on an inquisition.

"Excuse me. Mommy, can we go home and see Daddy?" Adam requested, anxious to leave.

Thankful for the interruption, I squeezed Adam and affected a look of apology in Ms. Debbie's direction, careful not to make eye contact. "We should be getting home."

"Have a blessed evening," she said as we departed. "We can talk another time."

"Not if I have anything to do with it," I muttered under my breath. I smiled and nodded respectfully and headed through the exit doors.

Turning to face me as he secured his seat belt, Adam asked, "Mommy, isn't Jesus God's son?"

"Yes, he is," I said.

He watched me, not hiding his confusion. "Why aren't you speaking to him? The people at Grandma's church say that He is everything. I mean really everything." His eyes became large like saucers when he said **everything.** I guess he wanted to emphasize that one word.

"To Grandma and the people that talk to him, He is everything. As for me, you and your daddy are everything." I bugged my eyes mimicking him and laughed.

"You look funny," he told me through giggles. "Grandma says that Jesus should come first and that we should always talk to him."

"That's fine for Grandma." Knowing that I had to tread lightly, I focused my attention on the road desperately seeking a diversion.

Seek ye first the kingdom of heaven...

I knew that Adam noticed me looking around but it was as if the voice was coming from inside of me.

Focusing my attention on turning into the driveway I noticed that Justin's car was there.

"Oh, look, there is Daddy's car; it looks like he is home a little early.

Why don't we ask if he wants to go out to eat?" I remembered that I had just cleaned the kitchen and really didn't feel like making a mess. We could eat leftovers from yesterday tomorrow. "Whatcha think?" I asked him, trying to pump him up.

"Yeah! Let's go to Ruby Tuesday's," he cheered.

Mission accomplished, I thought.

"Let's see where Daddy wants to go," I said, hoping that Justin wouldn't be averse to eating out.

I really needed to have a stress-free evening.

Upon entering the house, Adam greeted Justin and I have to admit that I was secretly pleased that his greeting continued to be a little lower than mine on the Richter scale. I knew that he loved his father but there was just something about a momma and her boy. Thankfully, Justin was in the mood to eat out but we decided on the Olive Garden.

During dinner, I noticed that Justin was a little pensive and didn't have too much to say. After getting Adam to bed, I joined him in the family room to see if I could get him to talk.

I placed my knees under my chin and snuggled next to him while placing my head on his chest. This was one of my favorite ways to sit with Justin. I guess that I felt protected and based upon on how I had been feeling lately, it was just what I needed. The emptiness returned whenever I allowed myself to reminisce or think about my life.

He was watching ESPN but he placed his arm around me instinctively.

"What's up?" I asked, trying to follow what was being discussed on television.

"Nothin'. How are you doing?" He looked down at me and I saw preoccupation in eyes but his voice seemed to convey genuine interest.

"You didn't have much to say at dinner. Didn't you want to eat at Olive Garden?"

"What? Oh yeah. It's just that I was thinking about work but it's all good. I don't have to travel but it is going to be a hectic couple of months. I am just not looking forward to it."

"I understand all too well," I empathized.

As I enjoyed the warmth that his body produced, I felt myself becoming a little sleepy but tried unsuccessfully to fight it. Deciding to give up the ghost, figuratively of course, I pushed back from Justin's chiseled chest and asked, "Do you mind if catch a few zz's here? I'm not really ready to get into the bed."

I snuggled closer to him and closed my eyes. He was always so warm. It was as if I was meant to stay there with him forever. If only I'd allow my heart to be at ease with him as easily as I allowed my body. Hurts and disillusionment occupied too much of my heart to truly be what I would call free, even with my own husband.

"Sure. I'll wake you when I turn in," he said, giving my shoulder a squeeze.

Justin seemed to always want to make me happy. He certainly had his flaws but I was happy that we found each other. There had been some rocky times. Times when I just knew that we wouldn't make it through the next week. It's not that I didn't love him because he was the only man that I'd ever want to marry. I knew that my distant behavior was taking its toll on our marriage but we seemed to continue to make it work. The question was, for how long? His patience with me was what made me love him so much. I knew that he was concerned about me. Sometimes he just wished that I would let him completely in. I tried, but my disappointments, not with men specifically but people in general, kept me from doing so. Hopefully one day soon, I'd muster enough strength to show him how much he meant to me, no holds barred.

We met when I was younger and a little bit more resilient. I realized now that my guard was up even at that time. For some reason, probably because of my youth and the novelty of our relationship, I was able to give him more of me. I know that I had begun to pull back. I needed to stop but couldn't control it. I was at risk of losing the only man that I knew was meant for me and only me.

It was the beginning of my senior year of college and I had just ended a long-distance relationship with a young man that was being groomed for the ministry. At the end of summer, I found out that he was cheating on me and decided against men in the church. Both of my closest girlfriends were in relationships which would have left me a little lonely but I was going to be a resident advisor and was president of a couple of college auxiliaries, the gospel choir and the newly organized black student union, just to name a few. I wasn't very concerned about my social life, as I knew that I was going to be pretty busy.

I really wanted to meet my husband while at college and could even recall that prayer request at the beginning of my college career. My relationship with Jesus had been deteriorating quickly during that time but I was trying to hold on. At least I thought so.

Justin was a transfer junior and I happened to walk right into him during a orientation mixer. I was looking down and not ahead of me when carrying boxes to the choir's table to set up. I was late as usual. I saw that the AKA table had free cookies and I was trying to get over there to get Karlie to slide me a few.

"Excuse me," he said. We seemed to lock eyes.

"Oh, I am sorry," I responded, not being able to tear myself away from his gaze. "I should have been looking where I was going and not making a bee-line for the free cookies." I laughed and tried to sound nonchalant. I could feel my smile getting wider.

Realizing that I was beginning to feel a little uncomfortable and couldn't think of anything to say, I immediately started with my choir spiel. I remember thinking that I sounded like one of the deacons from my church talking to a non-member about the church. I had no idea until that time that we sounded like a used car salesman. Did any of us believe what we were saying about God's goodness or even the good news of Jesus?

"I am assuming that you are a new student and I would like to invite you to the Inspirational Choir meeting this coming Sunday night. You don't have to join, just come and see what we are about. We are a gospel choir that just wants to spread the good news of Christ through song. We are pretty good. People don't expect our choir to be any good because the college is ninety percent Caucasian but the choir is one hundred percent African-American and we can sing."

He looked at me with an amused smile. His eyes were beautiful. That may sound like a weird way to describe a man's eyes but that is exactly what came to mind. Beautiful.

"Okay, you've convinced me to drop in. I can't promise that I'll join but I'll be there." He sounded like he meant it. His voice had a nice timbre. He didn't have the deep voice that reverberated in your chest but his voice was soothing. I liked the way his eyes never left mine and he had the sweetest smile.

"My name is Paige Hunter and I am a resident advisor in Roosevelt Dorm. If you have any questions or need any help, you can call me. I am in the campus phone book," I told him, extending my hand.

"Thanks. I'm Justin Covington," he said, taking my hand into his. His hands were large and I liked the rugged feel.

He has worked with his hands, I thought. I looked up at him and took note that he was about six feet two inches and very well-built. He had short wavy black hair styled in a fade. He had a football player's physique. I was puzzled for a moment. What was he doing here? This college didn't have a football team.

Thankfully, Justin certainly didn't seem like a dumb jock.

I noticed my girls, Karlie and Shara, waving to me so I smiled and nodded.

I looked at Justin and he was grinning at me. He obviously saw the exchange between my friends and I. I decided that making a quick exit before I embarrassed myself any further would be a good idea.

"See ya Sunday?" I asked, as I began to walk away, hoping that my question would be received as a confirmation.

"I give you my word," he stated and placed his hand on his broad and toned chest all the while continuing to smile at me.

"Night, Justin."

Chapter 4

My eyes opened to find Adam standing at the side of my bed looking quizzically at me. I returned the look as I slowly sat up and supplemented uneasiness to my demeanor. He was standing in his underwear. I guess he had an accident and wanted some help changing his sheets but was a little apprehensive about waking me. Justin must have helped me get to bed because I didn't remember even changing my clothes.

"Hey, sweetie," I said groggily as I swung my feet over the bed and wiggled my pink painted toes into my slippers. I was always amazed at how soft these slippers felt. They were a gift from Karlie. They said, "Walking with Jesus." I promised her that I'd wear them. This promise was made under protest.

I checked the illuminated digital clock on my night stand and it read 2:22 a.m. Justin had his back to me sleeping deeply.

"Mommy, can you help me?" Adam asked, looking at me with brown gumdrops for eyes.

"Sure. Are you okay?"

He nodded. "You were talking, Mommy. You were saying that it is all a show. Were you watching TV and fell asleep like Daddy?"

"I don't think so, baby. I was sitting with Daddy until he went to sleep. Let me go to the bathroom and I'll help you, okay?"

"Okay," Adam said and walked toward the linen closet to retrieve clean sheets. As I closed the door to the bathroom, I saw Adam standing on his toes pulling down Toy Story sheets.

I wondered what I was dreaming about. It's all a show? It must have been some television program that found its way into my dreams.

I flushed the toilet, washed my hands and reached under the sink to get the antibacterial cloths to wipe down Adam's vinyl mattress cover. I entered Adam's room and saw that he had put on a new pair of pajamas and was struggling with putting on the replacement pillowcase.

I offered to help him and then together we tackled the task of changing the sheets. Once completed, I washed my hands and allowed him get in the bed.

Kissing his forehead, I asked, "Did I say anything else while I was sleeping?" Watching him, I arrived at the conclusion that trying to figure out this dream was a challenge that I was not up to at the moment. I was ready to get back to bed.

"Nope. You said that it was all a show and that you don't want to be like them. Who were you talking about?" He was scooting down in the bed but his eyes didn't leave me as if he felt that he would miss something that my eyes would only communicate.

"Really?" I said, still confused about what my dream could have been.

"Yup. I am going to go back to sleep, Mommy," Adam said as he placed his head on the pillow and closed his eyes. His eyelids were already covering his eyes and the long eyelashes that he'd inherited from his father sealed them shut.

"Sleep well, baby," I whispered as I kissed his bitable cheeks.

"Uhmm," was his response as I left the room. I always left the door open. I never could understand how some parents could close the door of their child's room. I guess it's a Caucasian behavior because I didn't know any African-American parents who even allowed closed doors in their house unless that room was the bathroom.

As I slipped off my slippers and crept quietly under the sheet and comforter, Justin turned and garbled, "Everything alright?"

I snuggled close to him realizing that it was a little chilly but didn't want to alter the central air temperature. I hated making any changes to that system. I seemed to throw everything off kilter when I adjusted the settings.

"Yes, everything is okay."

His body heat was the best sleep aid that I could ever have. As I tuned out his snoring, I allowed my body to drift off to sleep but in my mind the words, "It's all a show," continued to play over and over.

I was at the church of my youth. The church was well attended and I noticed that my eldest sister, Darlene, was sitting in the presiding minister's chair. Her back was to me because I was in the choir loft with the rest of the choir. She turned around in anticipation and smiled in my direction. It was my cue and I moved to the microphone as I had been told that I was about to lead a song. The realization came to me as if someone whispered the secret in my ear. Although I was dreaming, I was participating and reliving a memory. A very vivid memory.

The song was "Answer Me" recorded by Dorothy Norwood. I remembered that my father liked when I sang this song. As a matter of fact, he requested that we sing this song. I realized that this was a special program and that last night I practiced this and another a song at church to ensure that our performance was perfect because Grandmother Hunter was visiting from Mississippi and I wanted to be great. As I walked to the microphone, I heard my choir mates say, "You better sing, P." I looked back and smiled knowing that they had confidence in me. I convinced myself that I was going to sing this song better than Ms. Norwood could.

The piano and organ began. The drummer joined in providing the beat and the choir started. I could feel that I was truly seeking an answer from Jesus.

"Answer me, please Jesus. Don't you hear me calling you? I need you, Lord."

The choir sang the chorus. When they sang the chorus the second time, I began to ad lib and then I sang the verse. As soon as I began, my voice seemed to be truly anointed. I sang the words in spirit and truth as that was the way I was taught to worship the Lord. As I sang the song,

I earnestly asked the Lord to answer me. I looked at my father in the audience. He seemed to be so proud of me but just last night he hurled so many accusations my way simply because I arrived home a little late from practice. One of the choir mothers, Mrs. Johnson, brought me home but that didn't seem to make a difference. He seemed not to care that I was practicing the song for tonight's performance. Who could I have been with?! I arrived home at 9:30 p.m. None of us considered this to a big deal. We were only at church singing. The choir director, Marvin, as well as Tommy, Kim, Saul and Mrs. Johnson, were there. After practice, we went to McDonald's for something to eat.

As I continued to sing, I felt the hot tears of hurt that the audience mistook for "the spirit" cascading down my cheeks. I sang the second verse, ad libbed the chorus with the choir and took the choir into what we called the vamp or run of the song. Continuing to sing, I remembered hearing the searing words of my grandmother that seemed to fuel my father, which resulted in him hitting me. A slap across my face was the gratitude that I received and ultimately my reward for trying to be the best. My mom was shouting at him the entire time but he didn't seem to hear her. All he heard was his mother. I couldn't believe that my dad had actually listened to my grandmother's conjured lies that hadn't any resemblance to fact or truth. When my head returned from the impact of being forced to the extreme left, courtesy of my father's large hands, my eyes began to sting with tears of bewilderment. My face felt hot and all I could do was stare at my dad. My mother finally stopped my father by grabbing his hand. She led me into the bathroom and tried without success to console me.

"Paige, I don't know what got into him," she whispered to me as she placed a warm washcloth on my cheek. "His mother…when she looks at you, sees your cousin and the way she is ruining her life in Mississippi and thinks that is what you'll wind up doing as well. She's an old woman but that does not give her the right to cause this havoc in my home." She stopped and just stared at me. She could see the pain in my eyes. Mom dabbed the cloth, now cold, onto to my cheek. I winced and turned my head.

"I know that you have never given us a reason not to trust you."
My cousin in Mississippi was only two years my senior. Grandma thought that she was ruining her life. Lilly had a baby and the father of the child was in jail. As children we were very close and I always knew that she was very intelligent. She simply lacked a little direction. Her parents were so caught up in their church life because my uncle was a minister, that they seemed not to have any interest in what was going on in Lilly's life. It was clear that something very wrong was going on. This was another reason why I had no stomach for "church life." As for Lilly's pregnancy, a baby is not a bad thing. Lilly did seem a little unstable. There was definitely a self-esteem issue present that was leading to bad choices. I wondered why I was being punished for Lilly's mistakes.

"Mother Hunter is leaving the morning after the church program tomorrow and I hope that she never comes back!" Mom screamed, knowing that my dad could hear her.

The dream once again shifted back to the actual performance.

I was walking out into the audience as we continued to sing. The entire church was on their feet. Grandmother looked as though she was having a conniption fit. I guess that was supposed to be her version of the Holy Ghost. Even my father was clapping with a smile on his face as he surveyed the audience behind him as if they were enjoying something that he'd done or even had a hand in. The choir director motioned to the organist to cut the accompaniment and only the drum beat remained.

"Answer me! Answer me, Lord! Answer me! Answer me, Lord!"

The place was jumpin'. The choir, with the help of the Lord, was turning it out. We ended the song and I made my way to my seat. The music returned and a mini reprise started.

My eyes scanned the crowd and I saw my mom. She was nodding her head in approval.

I looked at my grandmother being serviced by the nurse's aide. "What a phony. I'll never understand how you could have done that to me," I said, barely audible.

My eyes found my father's and I glowered at him. In my heart I promised him, *I will* **NEVER** *forgive you.*

After the program, I sat in back of the multipurpose room eating cake with some of my friends and choir members. We were laughing and talking about the program. Some of the church members and visitors came over and sat with me. They told me how much they enjoyed the choir's selections. I appreciated the accolades and had learned to easily discern genuine compliments from ones that were not. As my father made his way over with a few of the other deacons, my countenance changed and I am pretty sure that he noticed it. Knowing that I had to play the role, I summoned my "character" and greeted them.

"Deacon Hunter, you know that this daughter of yours can truly sing," Deacon Owens said with a smile while giving me a quick hug.

"Thanks, Deac. She is always practicing. She makes us proud," my father responded without looking at me.

I felt what seemed like a tidal wave in my abdomen and my eyes darted in the direction of the nearby restroom. As I stood, I graciously thanked Deacon Owens and excused myself. I walked quickly into to the ladies' restroom and looked into the mirror after allowing the feeling of nausea to subside. Disgust masked my sixteen-year-old face, and I whispered, "It's all a show."

Chapter 5

The end of the week arrived quickly. I mistakenly thought Friday was Saturday. Wishful thinking I guess. Justin helped me out and dropped Adam at day camp while I tried to get my day started. Only one more day and the weekend would be here.

Sitting at my desk I recalled the words that my son stated and I consciously computed the mental math, which resulted in my understanding of what he said and my subsequent dream. I must have been dreaming of those events all night. When exactly, I wondered, did I arrive at the understanding that it was all a show for some people in those days? I hadn't thought about that aspect of my childhood in many years. It is funny how one can simply choose to forget those events that caused them pain and confusion.

I remembered how I was able to perfectly imitate the deacons that prayed for what seemed like an hour on one knee in the front of the church, saying essentially the same thing. I often wondered how these men, who had to be up in age, possibly seventy years of age and over, were able to stay in that position for such a long time.

I leaned back in my chair and the word "Pharisee" came to mind. I simply couldn't understand why there was so much grandstanding. There was always an introduction to a prayer as if they were playing the piano intro before the actual song began. "Father, I stretch my hand to Thee…." Did God need to hear all of that? Didn't he already know what you were going to ask? Did He really care how eloquently one stated what their needs were or what they were thankful for? One of the Gospels told us how to pray and I didn't recall that we needed a great deal of drama. The use of what they thought was lofty terminology or flowery wording wasn't referenced at all. Weren't we all supposed to make it plain? I laughed aloud recalling the synonymous endings that were the same no matter where you went or who was praying. Something about a cooling board? I guess I had to realize that this was the way the elders, deacons and mothers of the church were taught to pray. At least some of them. I really believed that some really meant to be reverent but many were simply praying to hear themselves talk, all the while forgetting that they were speaking to God. Didn't they realize that He was supposed to already know their hearts? Foolishness, pure and simple.

I shook my head and found myself smiling at the memories, realizing that I had spent too much time thinking about that nonsense. Thank goodness I didn't have to worry about being in the midst of that circus. I made up my mind years ago that if that is what being close to Jesus was all about then I would stay as far away from God as possible.

But let every man examine himself…

"What?" I said to no one. Shaking my head, I decided that I was either tired or simply losing my mind.

Haven't I examined myself?

My outlook calendar rang and reminded me that I had a conference call at 11:30 and it was already 11:00 a.m. The voice had caught me off-guard. I tried to clear my head to try and catalog my time.

The call was with one of my clients and allowed just enough time for me to take a shower and throw a load of laundry into the washer. My day started a little behind schedule and early morning laundry had been skipped. I made a mental note to get a few loads in before the day was over. I hated when I started my day behind the eight ball. I didn't like waiting to take a shower late in the day but some things couldn't be helped. When I was late, everyone in the house was late. Although I was the one who didn't have to leave the house on a daily basis, I was still the crazy one running around trying to get everyone out of the door. Saturday couldn't get here soon enough.

Rather than taking the quick shower, I started following up on some communication projects that I sent to the marketing staff the week before to get a status on their completion dates. Because I worked with benefits and human resources vice presidents and administrators to ensure that they were satisfied with the service and assistance their employees received from the company, I never knew what my day would dictate, exactly. This was especially true during the planning and strategizing stages of benefits open enrollment. Not only was I required to continue to service the client and perform pro-actively to make a positive impact but also during this time, education and membership empowerment were the order of the day. Every client required a different educational strategy for enrollment. Most of my accounts decided not to make any changes. BHN was not really monetarily competitive but I had to admit that the service and e-technology that was offered surpassed many of the top carriers in the industry. A number of my accounts offered BHN alongside another healthcare carrier to provide choice. We were, for the most part, the more expensive option.

There was a lot that I had to do to prepare for open enrollment, which was typically held the last quarter of the calendar year. I had to travel a great deal to my clients' various locations. The creation of benefit presentations and communication pieces were also my responsibility. I was the lead for the execution of all client material. Many of my clients had numerous locations and because I was not able to attend all of the meetings scheduled by the client, I usually asked my counterparts across the country to assist unless the client specifically asked that I attend. My schedule usually didn't permit this rarity and the clients usually understood and found that most of my counterparts were very capable. Because it was already August, I really needed get plans solidified and receive client approvals for my accounts that were changing their designs. One account, Rosenfeld Data, decided to offer the new product and there were two that had decided to make slight benefit changes. The rest of my accounts were not altering their benefit designs and had decided not to make any increases with regard to employee payroll deductions.

I was certainly not looking forward to my strategy meeting with the people at Rosenfeld next week. After much negotiation with the decision-maker of their organization, Myra was successful in persuading them to offer the new consumer product that was coincidentally being offered across the industry. Rosenfeld contacted Leann, my teammate, and Myra, the team lead, to inform them that they had decided to change to the new health reimbursement arrangement product and had requested a sample of a presentation that would be used at an enrollment meeting. Their benefits department and employees as a whole, from what I had been told, were hard to satisfy so I had to really take the necessary time needed to explain the product to all levels of their employee base. Traveling two hours to get ripped a new one if I was not successful was not on my agenda. Myra had a good relationship with Rosenfeld's decision-maker, Carl Silver, VP of Benefits. I hoped to receive some pointers on what required emphasis in the presentation when we had our prep call. I made a mental note to work on the presentation when the house was quiet.

My reminder rang at 11:30 and I dialed into the conference call. I immediately placed myself on mute once indicating to all that I had joined and listened.

Not being able to decide what to make for dinner, I settled on a very generic salad, grilled steak for Justin and ziti for Adam and me. Adam usually liked sausage and ground sirloin in his ziti but we'd just have ground sirloin because we didn't have any Italian sausage in the house. If I planned my travels just right, I could put the ziti in the oven to bake while I went to camp to get Adam and be back in time to grill the streak for Justin.

Getting a couple of loads of laundry completed earlier proved helpful as well. That evening, after putting a few slides together for my presentation, I planned to fold the colored clothes while watching TV. I had become pretty good at multi-tasking home life and business.

Clicking "send" to transmit my last e-mail, I took another few moments to gather my thoughts for what needed to be done that night and the next day. I began to think of my mother and all of the things that she was able to get done and still raise us. I really wanted to talk to her again. I don't think that I was clear on the crux of my problem. I don't think that I even knew if I could even fully illustrate the gravity of the matter. It seemed that she had always been there to provide some type of direction even when it wasn't solicited. I knew that she felt that I should be a little closer to my father but some things take time. I had never been one to forgive easily. She'd always tell me that if Christ could forgive his own people for crucifying him, then we should be able to forgive anyone and everything.

"Easier said than done, Mom," I said aloud.

She gave God so much credit for the things in her life. Unfortunately, she didn't seem to remember the hypocrisy and lies she and the rest of my family witnessed and lived through at the hands of those people who called themselves Christians. My father was one of those people. To the outside world, we seemed like a glorious family. From the outside looking in, he was the most upstanding Christlike person, but I grew up watching this person and couldn't seem to equate Christ with the life that he showed us behind closed doors. He was not the only one. The people in my church, some of them anyway, were the exact same way. I thought of Ms. Debbie and her question. Do I know Jesus? Yeah, I know Him and all of His minions.

No thanks, I thought.

Some very good childhood friends ended up on drugs and in jail. We all grew up in church and reading the same bible. Is that what they got for spending all of their time in church? I am certain that we didn't have very good examples and I guess that I blamed all of the hypocrites and liars for the lives that they ruined.

*No, Paige, that is not who **I** am. Don't be deceived. They have chosen their own ways and their souls delight in their abominations.*

Okay. I didn't actually hear anybody speak but someone did speak to me and I was the only one in the house. My eyes swept my surroundings just to be sure. This was getting very unsettling.

Turning my attention back to dinner, I sprinkled the last of the mozzarella cheese on the ziti and placed it in the oven. Opening the fridge, I retrieved the steak. I seasoned it and poured Italian salad dressing on it to serve as a makeshift marinade. Using Saran wrap, I covered it and placed it back in the refrigerator. After washing my hands and slipping on my sandals, I scooped up my keys. I looked at the mirror to left of the front door for a quick once-over. I stopped and realized that my eyes were full of sadness. Was I happy? What a question to ask myself at 4:45 in the afternoon on a Friday. Most of the world in my position would have screamed, "Heck yeah!" I, unfortunately, didn't think so and I couldn't continue lying to myself. What was keeping me from true happiness or at least contentment? As I stared at the mirror, the reflection was replaced by my image at age eighteen. I then realized that I hadn't been truly and completely happy since around that age or maybe a little younger. That was when I began to see people as they truly were.

There were definitely some events that occurred later that certainly shaped me but I am convinced that my church life, unlike any secular events, set the stage for my awakening.

As I turned the key in the ignition, I once again viewed my reflection in the rearview mirror. My mind traveled back to when a bomb was dropped that undoubtedly broke the camel's back.

The Sunday before I left for my first year at college was one that I will never forget.

"Paige, are you up yet?" my mom screamed from the foot of the stairs. "You haven't finished packing and we are still going to church today!"

"I'm up, Mom!" I said, quickly checking my response, not wanting my annoyance to show. I didn't want to attend church but selfishly my father wanted me to go so that I could get some last minute "envelopes" to help with college expenditures.

"Take a bath," Mom said, as she approached my room. She seemed to have sprinted up the stairs. "You'll be taking enough showers once you are at school." Mom was of the old school. She believed in an old-fashioned bath and thought that a shower was the lazy way of washing oneself.

"Okay, Mom, I'll take a nice hot bath just for you."

"Don't do it for me, do it because you need to," she said, holding her nose and laughing as she disappeared into her bedroom. She was already bathed and was turning into her bedroom to get dressed for church service.

"Don't even try it, Mom," I said, sliding through the bathroom entrance. I turned the faucets of tub and placed a little bubble bath into the running the water. She was a trip.

Ida Olivia Hunter was and is a beautiful woman. Her hair was jet black and it always seemed to have an everlasting sheen. Her eyes were expressive when she regarded you. Many have said that they felt as if she could read your mind because her eye contact was just that intense. I think of bronze when I try to describe her complexion. Her skin was smooth and flawless except for some hereditary facial hair that I have as well. She is not a large woman but not small either. Mom was and is definitely a no-nonsense kind of woman and hasn't any patience for foolishness but will give you her last to ensure your safety and happiness.

As I exited the bathroom, my sister Celia almost knocked me over to get in.

"Jesus, girl, knock me over next time."

"Sorry but I had to go," she said, unconcerned.

"You could have knocked and just come in while I was in the bath," I said. True to form at that time of her life, Celia was always thinking of herself.

"I said that I was sorry but I couldn't wait," she huffed.

"Whatever," I said with an exasperated sigh, knowing that I wasn't going to win this argument.

Once I finished dressing, I surveyed my reflection. Mom had just pressed my hair the night before and I wore a simple sleeveless pink sheath dress. It complemented my youthful figure. I lined my lips and applied a light touch of fuchsia color. I didn't consider myself drop-dead gorgeous but was happy with myself. My hair had sheen like Mom's. I used a pick to style my hair that held what seemed like thousands of curls and decided that I'd better get moving.

My packing had been completed about a day ago and looking at my room, I realized that I was well-organized and ready to go. I promised Mom that I would vacuum my room so that nothing would be left on my plush mauve carpet.

As I descended the stairs, the smell of fried chicken, collard greens and sweet potatoes took my senses captive. Mom had cooked for my departure. Thank You Jesus! I was hoping that we would eat at home before we left for school.

"Mom, you didn't have to do all of this," I lied as I glanced around the kitchen noticing the potato salad and corn bread mix. My eyes became as big as bowling balls when I spied the peach cobbler out the corner of my eye, sitting on the counter. I absolutely loved peach cobbler.

"Yes, I did. We all have to eat but I wanted you to have a good home-cooked dinner before you left."

I kissed her on the cheek. Her skin was so soft. She was always looking out for me.

We arrived at church in what seemed like a whirlwind as a result of a telephone call that Daddy received right after we finished breakfast. We could all tell that it upset him. He slammed the receiver down and left the room. There were rumors of congregational unrest after the last church conference and accusations of embezzlement had been flying around the church for most of the summer. During the conversation, he invited another deacon, Deacon Gerry, to our house for dinner. I, of course, didn't appreciate this supposed act of generosity because I wanted this to be only family but then again it was only Deacon G. He was very upset with our pastor for some reason and had not made his disappointment and dissatisfaction a secret. He had even talked about resigning from the deacon board. That sent a big message to the congregation and as a result, the gossips were off and running.

New Light Baptist Church was located across town, right across from a seedy bar and hotel. The church had been in existence for approximately seventy-five years and its history of pastors was legendary. It was a beautiful building and the membership was considered quite large at the time. There were about 1,000 members but only 500 were regular attendees.

It seemed that there was always something going on that kept new membership away. The ones that didn't attend never left to join another church but simply stayed away and attended on the major holidays: Christmas, Resurrection Sunday and sometimes Mother's Day.

It always seemed that Daddy needed to be in the center of what was going on so we left the house in quite a hurry. I don't know why he insisted on all of us driving together knowing that we wanted to leave directly after service. He always stayed to supposedly talk to the members and other deacons. He drove with noticeable speed and when we pulled into the parking space, he jumped out of the car as if something bit his backside.

"I'll see you inside," he murmured to Mom and headed inside with a quick gait that turned into a jog.

"What is going on, Mom?" I asked. I wasn't all that surprised by Dad's need to get inside but this morning he seemed in a silent frenzy because he wasn't fussing all the way to church; his usual behavior. She shrugged her shoulders. I looked at her closely and noticed that she was avoiding eye contact. This was something that Mom never did unless she didn't want to tell you something.

We stopped going to Sunday school some time ago so we were a little early for morning service. I entered the vestibule with the customary greetings, embraces and handshakes and went directly to the descending stairs that led to the restrooms to once again check my appearance.

My sisters joined me in the bathroom after a few moments. Our demeanors were masks of confusion but no one said anything for the moment.

"I am just glad I am going back to school on Wednesday. It is getting so that I don't want to come home anymore," Loni said, breaking the silence and verbalizing what we all felt.

"I could have worked in D.C. this summer but felt obligated to come home to work because of Mommy," Celia confessed.

I said nothing. Anything that I wanted to say was already being communicated through my eyes. My oldest sister was so lucky that she received an opportunity to travel abroad and not have to contend with the craziness that this summer had afforded the rest of us.

Suddenly, a woman burst into the bathroom. She had visibly been crying. Her mascara streaked her pecan-colored skin. I recognized the woman. She was Maya Matthews. I was certain that it was Maya. I knew her and her family. Her father was one of the deacons.

"Maya, what is the matter?" I asked as I walked over to the double sinks where Maya was dampening a paper towel.

She acknowledged me but said nothing at first and then she groaned, "Deceitful…"

I looked back at Celia and Loni. They shook their heads. Loni, being the concerned citizen that she had always been, gestured for me to inquire further.

"What is going on, honey? Here, sit down." I motioned for Maya to sit down next to me on one of the high-backed cushioned burgundy chairs. Loni and Celia remained standing next to the door as if standing guard.

"Paige, I can't talk about it now but you'll certainly be hearing about it," she said through sniffles. I looked at Maya and realized that her eyes were beet red and there was a small bruise under her left eye. Maya was an attractive young lady. Her burnt orange curly ringlets cascaded past her shoulder. A lone curl hid the light brown eye with the unattractive blue and black decoration. I placed my hand on top of hers and stated that whatever it was, it was going to be okay.

She shook her head violently and began to cry even harder and louder. The pain that she felt, whether emotional or physical, seemed to originate from down deep within.

I hugged her and asked if she needed anything. She managed to say no and thanked me. I secretly resolved to send a nurse's aide to the bathroom just to make sure.

"I don't want to leave you like this, Maya," I admitted, becoming increasingly worried about her. She hadn't stop crying since she entered the bathroom.

"You, Loni and Celia can go, I'll be okay. The worst is yet to come," she mumbled into her paper towel that was crumbled in the hand that covered her mouth. Her hands were visibly shaking.

"Okay." Not knowing what else to say, we left the bathroom. I found Sister Wise and asked her to the check on someone in the bathroom. I dared not tell her that it was Maya.

As we entered the sanctuary and moved to take our usual seats toward the back, the air seemed thick like a storm was brewing. The devotional and testimonial portion of service was all but completed and the choir was in place for their procession.

It could have been my imagination but no one was looking directly at the pulpit when Pastor Simon stood to address the congregation.

I looked at Celia and asked, "What is up?"

"I don't know, girl, but we are about to find out." She turned and pointed to the door as it flew open and Deacon Matthews, Maya's father, ran down the aisle toward the pulpit.

"You demon!" he shouted. "You are supposed to be a man of God." His eyes were moist, ready to spill the liquid mixture of immense anger and betrayal.

The church became as quiet as a morgue. The rest of the deacons except for Deacon Owens started moving tentatively toward Deacon Matthews. They moved slowly with trepidation. Either they secretly wanted this drama to play out or they were really afraid of what Deacon Matthews was going to do.

Matthews jumped onto the pew to his left as if he was a man thirty years younger and began to leap carefully but with determination from the back of each pew to the next in an effort to get toward the front of the church where Pastor Simon stood transfixed in sheer horror and fear.

The church was in the midst of mass confusion and chaos. Sister Highland, who sat right smack dab in the middle of the pew, was almost stepped on. Because she was older, she wasn't able to move out of the way fast enough.

She quickly removed her beautiful white hat and shouted, "Jesus, what is going on!?"

The deacons lost all decorum as they tried to head off Deacon Matthews. Sister Horne, one of the mothers of the church, was sitting on the floor crying, with her hands raised toward the heavens, asking the Lord to deliver her.

"Deliver her from what?" I asked myself aloud but certainly not loud enough for anyone to hear. This was a sight to behold.

"You were supposed to be a decent man. You said you loved her and this congregation and you do this? What kind of man are you?" Deacon Matthews wailed.

"Daddy!" Maya screamed and all heads turn to the back of the church. In the midst of all of the pandemonium, she began to walk toward the front of the church. "Don't put him on a pedestal. He is just a man and one of the worst kind. I walked in on him with some woman and she was treating him to all of her goodies." She looked at Pastor Simon with contempt and disgust. It was the kind of look you give a person right before you decide that you want to spit on them.

"You all know that we were engaged to be married," she continued, turning to address the congregation. "But it was all a lie." Maya arrived at the pulpit and stood at the foot of the three steps that separated the sanctuary from the raised "sacred area" and breathed audibly as if it was the most painful breath she ever exhaled. "I was determined not to run out when I saw what had been going on. I had to know the truth. That is something that my daddy taught me. When I confronted him in his study with the woman still naked on the floor and on her knees, he laughed." Her fingers traced the bruised eye and continued. "He has desecrated our church and our relationship with his behavior. The woman laughed at me and said that this man, your devoted and Holy Ghost-filled pastor, had been embezzling money from the church and had planned to leave town at the end of week. My eyes found their way to his desk and true enough; tickets to California were in plain sight. Apparently, not a very good thief or liar. My mind didn't want to process the venom she was spewing."

"Maya." Pastor Simon tried to speak, no doubt trying to defend his behavior. He was stepping toward her, hands outstretched in an effort to touch her and make it alright.

"No, Cleavon! You are a drunk and a liar and you have used everyone in this church!" Maya's tears returned as the dam broke once again. The byproducts of the pain, hurt and deception emptied from her eyes as her mother led her out of the sanctuary. She was leaning on Mrs.

Matthews for support and then she started to laugh. She threw her head back and laughed raucously. Everyone thought that she was losing her mind.

As we all watched Maya being taken out of the sanctuary, we heard a crack that sounded like lightning during a late summer thunderstorm. All of our heads snapped back to center stage to find that Deacon Matthews had reached Pastor Simon and successfully landed a Mike Tyson left-cross to his jaw. It was as if Pastor's fall was in slow motion. He finally kissed the carpet with a thud. Out cold.

After hearing and absorbing all that had transpired, it was my turn to be shocked and unable to move. I truly looked up to Pastor Simon. He had been to our house on many occasions. He had given me rides home and seemed to have a genuine interest in my relationship with Christ. Were all ministers like Pastor Simon? Weren't they? At that moment I remembered entering his study and finding him a little disheveled after his assistant, Sister Alfreda, left a bit too abruptly. I thought nothing of it at the time.

Daddy spent a great deal of time with Pastor Simon as well. Late night meetings and trips to conferences…Did Daddy know about his philandering and was Daddy a part of it? Did he take part? I was beginning to get a headache. My head started to pound right at the temples and I had to sit down. My church home was a lie and my real home had been under suspicion for some time and this added more fuel to the fire. Why would God allow so many people to be misled and hurt? I felt like the apostle Paul because the scales had begun to fall from my eyes.

Chapter 6

Karlie called and informed me that she would not be bringing Tara with her so I convinced Justin and Adam to spend the entire day together. I rose early Saturday morning to spruce up the guest room and guest bath. Only Adam used the bathroom but I wanted to make sure that it was more than appropriate for guests.

I had no idea what Karlie and I were going to do all weekend but it was just nice to have her coming to visit.

Scrubbing the bathroom tub was a chore that I absolutely abhorred but it needed to be done and I knew that I couldn't expect Adam or Justin for that matter to do it for me. I couldn't wait until Adam was able to clean up more or at least take on a few chores. As I was rinsing the cleanser from the side of the tub, Justin entered the bathroom.

"I smell something good. What are you making your men for breakfast?" he asked, eyes full of anticipation.

"It's only the bacon that you smell. I will make corned beef hash, eggs and grits for you and pancakes for Adam." He looked at me and grinned. I returned to my task of using the Mr. Clean Eraser to get anything that Comet missed.

"I guess that meets your approval." Without waiting for an answer, I added, "It should, because you know I don't really cook on the weekend. Karlie and I will probably go out for lunch when she gets here and won't eat anything of real substance for dinner. You know how much we love just eating sweets." I finally turned to face him and he had an expression of admiration mixed with apprehension painted on his features.

"What?"

"Your father called," he announced.

"Is there anything wrong?" I asked, not wanting to really speak to anyone or return anyone's call unless it was an emergency.

"It didn't seem so. He said that your mother was having a family dinner because your Aunt Dinah is visiting. I am sure that they want you to stop over for a bite to eat Sunday afternoon."

Our eyes locked and he recognized my look of reservation.

"I don't know. Why didn't Mom call me?" I said, a little incensed. I knew that he didn't have the answer but the question just spilled out.

"You know you need to go," he said, trying to be the voice of reason. A voice that wasn't welcome in this dialogue. I was hearing too many voices as it was.

"I don't want to go over there."

"He is your father, Paige. You don't know how lucky you are to have your parents alive. If I could have one moment with my mom and dad..." He turned to leave the bathroom, shaking his head.

He just doesn't understand, I rationalized.

"Karlie may not want to go over there," I said raising my voice so that he could hear me down the hall.

"Don't try and make excuses. You know they love Karlie. I'd like to try and understand exactly why you have come to hate your father so much. As long as we have known each other, you've always tensed up around him. You and the rest of your sisters. Paige, did he ever...touch you?"

"No, it is definitely not anything like that. I don't think he could ever do that but he was another kind of monster. Maybe monster is too harsh a word but that is how I viewed him. He was like a Dr. Jekyll-Mr. Hyde type personality to me."

My father, Evan Simeon Hunter, was a tall, intimidating man.

Standing at about six feet one inch, he was of average weight with a slight tummy. He tried to stay active for a man of his sixty-two years. His skin tone was the color of maple syrup. He was beginning to bald just enough for us to notice. Dad had dark eyes that were unreadable. His broad nose was his most distinguishing physical characteristic. His brow seemed always furrowed. It was as if he was always thinking. I can't remember him actually having an approachable demeanor. As a child, I remembered that he was involved in most of our activities. We even played baseball on a regular basis with the neighborhood kids. My relationship prior to junior high school seemed normal enough, or so I thought. Of course he was always the primary disciplinarian but my mom was no stranger to setting someone straight. I wondered what happened or what surfaced to make things change? Was I blind to his hypocrisy when I was a child?

He didn't talk much about his childhood or his life prior to meeting and marrying Mom. That always seemed pretty odd to me but then again, what did I know?

"Are you going to call him?" Justin prodded as he reappeared in the bathroom entryway. He knew how I was when I just finished cleaning a room, especially mopping. He dared not enter the area. I was a bit neurotic about a clean bathroom.

"I guess Mom is looking for me to make an appearance," I admitted grudgingly.

"That's my girl," he said, reaching for me. I abruptly shrank back, not wanting him to hug me or even touch me. I was oblivious as to why I couldn't produce a rational explanation for my behavior. I was repelled for a second. No, I was repulsed at the thought of going to my parents' home. I could feel that I was grimacing and tried to relax my expression but it was too late.

"What's wrong?" He looked at me with hurt in his eyes.

"Nothin'," I lied, realizing that I was still a little on edge.

"Why do you get this way? This is getting a little unnerving and annoying." He crossed his large chocolate biceps across his chest and looked at me. He frowned, noticeably unhappy with my decision to once again shun his affection or even his touch. I really didn't mean to be cold but it was just a reflex. An unhealthy reflex that was becoming the norm. I really needed to check myself.

"Justin, I am sorry." I was certain that he was more than a little annoyed with me. I wanted him to leave on a positive note and enjoy his day with Adam.

"I am going to take a shower. I'll get Adam ready so that we can eat," he said with a voice that led me to conclude that he was tired of the entire situation and me. He turned and left me standing in the bathroom with the mop in my hand, feeling like the fool that I was.

Breakfast was quiet except for Adam's constant jabbering about catching a baseball. He loved the sport and was very excited about the game. Our city had a triple-A team and we always tried to take in a couple of games during the season. I knew he was looking forward to his day with his father and I want badly to patch things up with Justin. He barely looked at me when fixing his plate. I could tell that he was really hurt by my behavior. He was right. This was becoming a habit.

Adam tore into his pancakes and had three slices of bacon. Thankfully, Justin mustered up his appetite to eat his breakfast as well.

I tried to catch Justin's eye while eating. When I finally caught them and retained eye contact, I felt like I was cleaving to a raft in the middle of the ocean and was holding on for dear life. I mouthed, "I'm sorry," flicked my tongue seductively and blew him a kiss. His eyes smiled but his mouth stubbornly decided not to surrender any signs of forgiveness. I had to make it up to him somehow.

He is so good for me, I said inwardly, *I can't alienate him.*

Sometimes it seemed as though I couldn't trust or love anyone except my child. Had I been provided with such a bad example of love that I couldn't truly give of myself or show love to anyone?

I am love. *I love you and have already proven it. Open your heart so that you can love again.*

This was getting to be creepy. The voice was not audible to the ear but I could hear it. Something had to be done, but what?

Karlie pulled into my driveway around noon, only an hour after my men left for a day of baseball. I hadn't realized how much I missed seeing my friend. She moved away when she married Tyson and it had been pretty difficult to see each other. Our friendship is one that truly stood the test of time. We met during my senior year of high school. She was a transfer senior. If that wasn't the worst part, her parents had just divorced and she was living with her mother who was very bitter. Her mother never let her go anywhere without her and when Karlie and I became friends, we never went anywhere without each other. We were like peanut butter and jelly. If I happened to be somewhere by myself, and anyone saw me, they'd customarily ask, "Where's K?" Karlie would tell me that she received the same type of inquiry. It was great to have a friend like her. I believed that we were destined to be "girls," because we hit off so well. With Karlie, I shared my thoughts and feelings about what I was slowly learning about my life. She understood that I was beginning to become confused about my parents' relationship. What I really treasured about our friendship is that we could really talk. We didn't have to walk around on eggshells. She was honest with me and I was the same with her.

What I thought I knew about God was constantly being shown to be untrue by the behavior I consistently witnessed. I think that was why Karlie and her mother never joined our church. I divulged too much information. I can't assume too much of the blame because there was always something going on that somehow found its way around the city. Mrs. Norriton, Karlie's mom, always found out the news. I guess that I just confirmed that what she heard was true.

As she walked up the cobblestone path leading to my front door, I noticed that her hair had grown. Had it been that long since I'd seen her? I always envied her hair. Karlie is a full-figured woman of about five feet five inches. She was always talking about losing weight. Her husband was known to say, "Only dogs want bones." Tyson could always make me laugh. As long as her husband thought that way, I didn't know how she was going to win that battle. Nevertheless, my job was to support her if that was what she was wanted to do. As she emerged from her car, the sun seemed to lightly kiss her sienna complexion. She had the perfect African-American nose; broad enough to emphasize her ethnicity, but not too broad. Her lips always had a touch of pink even if she didn't have on gloss. Her gray eyes were searching mine as she approached. I could see the concern and quickly averted my eyes until I could change my demeanor.

"It is so good to see you, sweetie," I said as we embraced and I kissed her on the cheek. I could smell the Mary Kay scent "Belara," another one of our common likes. She smiled but there was a vibe that I couldn't exactly put my finger on. Karlie was on a mission.

"Always, girl," she agreed.

"Come on in and we can get your bag a little later. Do you need anything out of it?" I asked, leading her into the house.

She shook her head and stopped suddenly.

"Paige, I love the colors," Karlie almost screamed as she whirled around in wonderment. She immediately walked into the living room and looked back at me with a smile that brought more sunshine into the house. "This is absolutely beautiful. Did you hire someone to do this?"

"Girl, now you know that we can't afford fancy-schmancy painters or decorators. Justin did all of the painting and I found the furniture. We worked together. Even Adam offered his two cents. It was fun," I confessed waving my hand around the room like Vanna White on *Wheel of Fortune.* "I just have to get to the kitchen."

"Wow! He did a great job. Paige, you have a gorgeous home, a loving husband, a sweet little boy." She walked into the family room and laughed. "And don't forget your health. Because if you have your health…"

"You've got everything," I joined in as we both finished my mom's familiar mantra.

"How dare you be unhappy," she said with a look of manufactured disappointment.

"That's just it. I have no reason to feel the way I do. What is missing, K?" I asked, giving her an expression similar to that of an inmate at Bellevue Mental Hospital. I realized that I sounded like one of those unfulfilled housewives that I saw on TV. Not exactly, because I did work outside the home. Okay, well not literally. In any case, I am not a housewife.

"Paige, deep down I think that you know what is missing or should

I say who is missing." Her countenance became serious and she sat on the lavender chaise. She looked at me and I could tell that she was about to drop some science on me. I was not sure that I wanted to hear what she had to say, but because she was my dearest friend, more like a sister, I decided that I would hear her out.

After an afternoon of shamelessly eating to our hearts' content and shopping past my limit, Karlie and I kicked around the possibility of taking in a movie.

"Why don't we sit at the house, take advantage of the fact that the guys aren't there and watch a movie on the big screen?" I said, feeling a wonderful sense of freedom.

"I am with that," she agreed with a girlish smile.

"Okay, *Pride and Prejudice*?" I asked, knowing that it was going to be either that or *Imitation of Life* starring Lana Turner.

"Don't tell anyone but I think Colin Firth is so handsome," she confided with a chuckle.

"Me too, girl. You know I'm not into white bread. Pumpernickel is more my preference but if he was the last man on earth, I wouldn't be too upset."

She held up her hand and said, "Alright now! Don't leave me hangin'!" I slapped her palm and we laughed all the way to the house.

That night, we didn't get to bed until about 2:00 a.m. Once finally retiring, I found myself next to Justin listening to the first movement of his snoring symphony that proved to be one for the books. It was always customary for Karlie and I to talk until the wee hours of the morning. I thought about the heart-to-heart conversation that Karlie and I had earlier that day. She did make some valid points.

My relationship with the people in past as well as my parents had dictated my relationship with my husband and some parts of my personality. Wasn't that normal? She, however had the gall to say that I didn't see or recognize the importance of Jesus in my life. She went on to say that I had just chosen not to recognize it. I knew that she was going to go there. She wouldn't be Karlie if she didn't mention something about God and His Son. She said that although it was good to look up to and admire people, it wasn't healthy because people would undoubtedly disappoint. She was certainly right about that. Almost everyone, from my previous pastors and my parents to the people that I thought were the most moral and God-fearing, had disappointed me in their deeds and actions. How could Jesus allow them to continue misrepresent Him and not do anything? Did Jesus care? If He didn't care about how He was being represented how could I be certain that He cared about me? Karlie didn't have answer to the first question. To the second, she pulled out her bible and read 1st Peter 5:7. She asked me to read it.

"Cast all your cares upon Him; for he careth for you." I looked up at Karlie and petal soft words were impressed upon my heart.

Just because you choose not to listen to Me doesn't mean that I will not stop talking to you or loving you. You have not chosen me but I have chosen you.

I decided not tell Karlie about the voice that I had begun hearing. I already knew her answer. Trying to live for Christ had already cost me too much pain and confusion.

"There are other places in the bible that indicate that Christ does care about you, Paige. You can't let wolves in sheep's clothing keep you from Christ. I have to say that this is the reason why I think that you are in a funk. I have been led to pray for you and I have been. I hope that you will take what I said to heart. You know my history and if I can find peace and arrive at a place where I know that I know, you can too. You can only find your true purpose and know what you are all about when you touch base and consult your manufacturer, and your manufacturer is God. He made you, Paige."

I smiled because I liked how she put that. Only Karlie could make it so plain.

She mentioned that she knew a co-worker who had a relative in my area and that she was a member of a church that was non-denominational. "The church is really bible-based. Although the pastor is African-American, they are not chained to traditions like so many are."

She walked into my kitchen and placed the information on the refrigerator with one of the BHN company magnets and said, "Give the church a chance. I know you haven't gone to service in while but do it as a favor me. You won't be disappointed. I heard the CD and the pastor is pretty good." She smiled and hugged me.

"Love you, girl," she said as she ascended the steps and walked into the guest bathroom.

Not wanting to think about the conversation any longer, I decided to get up and check on Adam. He arrived home, flying higher than he was when he left this morning. I walked quietly into his room and he was sleeping peacefully. A slight rumble with the makings of a snore escaped his lips. He was actually sleeping with a smile on his face. I envied that smile.

Chapter 7

Sunday morning greeted me with the smell of breakfast sausage. I rolled over and looked at the clock. It read 9:15 a.m. I guess I was tired from yesterday and the late night and didn't even realize it. It was so sweet of Justin and Adam to let me sleep in. We hadn't any plans this morning. Thankfully.

I sat up in bed as the rays of sun washed my face. It felt good. I closed my eyes and began to recall what Karlie said. Almost immediately I began feeling tense in my shoulders and decided not to think about it. Building up myself for further disappointment was not on my life's agenda.

"Mommy," sang a sweet voice attached to a brown little head with curly hair. Adam's smile would melt anyone's heart. He poked his head into the doorway.

"Yes, my prince," I said, not being able to suppress a grin.

"Good morning, sweet Mommy," Adam said as he completed a running jump onto to my bed.

Adam smiled and gave me a big kiss.

"Now that is what's going to make it a great morning," I said while giving him a big hug. I began to tickle him and he fell over onto his father's side of the bed, laughing and screaming. Once the screaming subsided, he informed me that he and Justin had made breakfast for K and I and that I should get up, brush my teeth and get downstairs because the food was on the table.

"Is Aunt Karlie up and did you give her the same message?" I inquired, beginning to tickle him again as he tried unsuccessfully to exit the bed.

"Yes, Mommy. Auntie K is already downstairs," he laughed. I looked at his beautiful face and decided that I wanted to have another child. I silently made a mental note to talk about this with Justin after Karlie left.

Over a breakfast of southern pork sausage, scrambled cheese eggs and bagels, we talked about the plans for the day and I admitted that against my better judgment, I returned my parents' call yesterday and that I would visit for an hour or two to say hi to my Aunt Dinah.

"I knew you had it in you," Justin said, sounding proud of me.

"May I go with you and Aunt K to see Grandma and Grandpa?" Adam asked. He really loved seeing his grandparents and he knew that Grandma Hunter always had something for him.

Before answering Adam's request, I wordlessly but visually consulted Justin to see if he would like to accompany us as well. He seemed to read my mind as well and told us that he had plans to mow the grass and do some yard work this afternoon so he wouldn't be able to join us. He also mentioned that he wanted Adam to help with a few things.

I looked at him with a pleading expression and he unmistakably responded with a look of his own. "No way."

I decided to stop at the bakery to pick up a carrot cake. Aunt Dinah loved carrot cake. After all, I couldn't just show up empty-handed.

"Karlie! It is so good to see you, dear," Mom said to Karlie as she gave her a warm hug. She stepped back to look at Karlie. "You look wonderful. I see that you have kept the weight off. Good girl."

"Thanks, Mrs. Hunter. I am doing my best but your daughter knows my vices and we have been awfully naughty this weekend. Please don't be offended if I don't eat too much. I am full from yesterday." Karlie looked at me and playfully pushed me.

"I didn't hold a gun to your head, girl. Mommy, if you've cooked, I am eating," I said, immodest.

I entered the house and an uncomfortable feeling tried to take hold but when I saw my Aunt Dinah it seemed to draw back just as darkness retreats when light is introduced.

I greeted Aunt Dinah with genuine warmth. I am told that she and I have similar personalities and that we also resembled each other. It was good to see that she was well. I sometimes wished she lived closer so that we could talk more often. She seemed to always understand my woes. Unfortunately her advice would probably be very similar to Karlie's.

Celia, Loni and Darlene were sitting in the dining room. Celia and Loni's husband were not in attendance either.

"Hey, guys," I said to the three in greeting.

"What's up, Paige?" they said in unison.

"Dad was wondering if you were going to make it," Celia said while lifting a forkful of collard greens to her wine-colored glossed lips.

I decided not to respond to her comment and turned to Karlie to ask if she wanted to get something to eat.

"I am just getting an extra small portion of a few of the dishes that your mom has cooked," she stated sheepishly.

I gently pulled her close to ensure that only she could hear my next statements. "You know I am about to throw down so don't make me look like a pig. I'll run it off tomorrow. Don't embarrass me, child."

Karlie giggled and nodded her head.

"Can I get anyone anything from the kitchen?" I asked as I looked around the table.

Negative responses were returned so I grabbed Karlie's hand and made my way into the kitchen.

As I stepped into the kitchen, Dad turned around and our eyes met. He quickly looked away and his gaze landed on Karlie and a smile emerged.

"Hi there, Ms. Karlie," my father said as he enveloped her in an embrace. "It is so good to see you. So I guess it took you and Dinah coming to town for Paige to visit her family," he verbally jabbed, looking at me over her shoulder and releasing Karlie from the hug. I guess the cloaked affront gave him the courage to now visibly regard me.

"I am sure that is not true, Mr. Hunter. Paige has been telling me that she has been doing a great deal of work that has monopolized all of her time," Karlie stated in my defense.

"I guess that may be true. At least she stays in touch with her mom by phone. I, on the other hand, have not seen or spoken to her for not longer than a hot second since the beginning of the summer," he reported, trying to draw blood from the wound.

"Why are you guys talking about me as if I am not even in the room?" I asked, a little irked. I attempted to keep it out of my voice. I suppressed my annoyance with a smile. "What's up, Dad?" I said.

"Same old thing, Paige. Didn't you bring my little partner with you?" He inquired after Adam.

"No. I decided that Adam needed to stay with his dad to help with the yard work. Did you and Mom take Aunt Dinah to church this morning?" I knew that if I talked about his beloved church, the conversation would be a little bit more to his liking.

"Yes, today was communion. You know that the new pastor doesn't allow the deaconess to hold the cloth anymore and only the deacons, assistant pastor and pastor can now perform the task. The ladies don't appreciate being relegated to the task of just washing out the wine glasses. There was a little push back. Of course your mother wasn't concerned but some made their objections known to me and asked if I could talk to the pastor about it." He seemed to boast about the fact that he had the ear of the pastor and that the congregation thought that his words might hold some weight. His chest even looked as if it was protruding to physically make his point. I had to be imagining that.

"I am certain that everything will work out," I said, not wanting to place any more importance on this matter. New Light had not shaken its need for tradition. I didn't recall that communion was such a big production in the bible. I certainly knew its necessity and what it symbolized. To change the process or not change was too big a deal and all of the unrest surrounding this would undoubtedly completely takeaway its real importance.

"Why are you shaking your head?" Karlie and my dad seemed to ask me almost in harmony.

"Oh, nothing. It just seems that things don't change," I admitted with a wry smile.

"You should come back. I am sure that you could help and make some changes. Everyone is always asking me about you," Dad said, using a coaxing tone usually reserved for the church members.

"No offense, Dad, but there is no way I would ever go back to that church to become a member," I stated with vehemence.

Dad looked a little taken aback by the conviction in my voice. His eyes seemed to reveal a little sadness and disappointment. The unchecked display of emotion quickly left his eyes. His shoulders quickly lifted and he turned his attention to Karlie. This was my opportunity to exit the conversation.

I feigned disinterest in their conversation as I filled my plate with all of the wonderful dishes that had been prepared. I felt a hand on the small of my back and turned and looked into the eyes of my mom. Her eyes told me what I already knew. "Take it easy on New Light and Daddy."

I returned the look with an unuttered, "I haven't said anything."

We left it at that. She must have overheard the conversation. I didn't want her day to become one of arguments or disagreements. She didn't get to see her sister that often and I decided that I'd eat and chat with Dinah and my sisters and shortly thereafter make my exit.

"Before you leave, I need to talk with you," she whispered.

"You sound funny, Mom. My trouble radar is sensing something," I said.

"No need to become alarmed, I just want to have a quick conversation with you," she said reassuringly with a motherly smile. She patted my hand and turned to Darlene who had just called her name.

I didn't like having "conversations" with Mom. I wondered if Celia, Darlene and Loni already knew what she was going to disclose.

Karlie joined me and her plate looked just as packed as mine. She had more macaroni and cheese on it than anything. I spied the ribs that she had on her plate as well. The meat was just falling off the bone.

I hadn't seen those ribs.

Exiting the kitchen, I made a mental note to get the ribs to go.

"What's all this whispering," she asked conspiratorially.

"Mom is being awfully mysterious," I said.

My mom must have overheard our discussion because she poked her head between us and whispered just loud enough for Karlie and me to hear, "No mystery. Enjoy and eat as much as you want." She pinched me playfully and walked away.

We spent the next two hours laughing and talking with Aunt Dinah and my sisters allowing Mom and Dinah to recall memories of their childhood. It was good seeing Mom enjoying her sister. They had always been close and I secretly wished that my sisters and I were as close as they seemed to be.

Dad entered the living room while Mom continued to talk about her humble beginnings and it was interesting that although Mom and Dad said that they were both poor, Mom never seemed to be haunted by that fact. Dad seemed to do everything in his power not return to that status or even talk about it.

Mom looked at me and moved her head inconspicuously in the direction of the sitting room at the front of the house.

I slowly rose out of my chair, excused myself, and followed her into the room, closing the French doors behind me.

"I am not going to get into it today, Paige, but come by the house later this week. We need to have a discussion and I think that it is long overdue."

"What kind of discussion, Mom?" I asked, not wanting to make the hour-long trip if I could just hear what she had to say today.

"You need to understand some things and I am at fault for not talking to you and your sisters about it sooner. I thank God each day that you have all married decent men and that you have retained your independence but there is something that I failed to pass on to you and it is better late than never. Today is a day for family but call me so that we can have lunch and talk, okay?" Her eyes seemed to plead with me to agree to meet with her.

"What does my choice in men or my life have to do with what you want to talk to me about?"

"It just does. Paige, I pray for you every day. It seems that I pray for you more than your sisters because something in my spirit tells me that you need to open your heart. To what, I am not sure. It is my most fervent prayer that you will eventually come to realize what it is and that you must release whatever has you bound."

I felt a little unnerved by her choice of words. "Mom, I am not bound by anything," I said defensively.

"Trust me, Paige, you are," she said with a voice that was both loving and firm.

Becoming uncomfortable with where the conversation is going, I began to look around the room. I looked out into the living room through the glass of the French doors and noticed that Dad was looking in our direction. I returned my attention to Mom, with my arms crossed defensively.

"Okay, I'll call you so that we can get together," I surrendered, wanting to leave the room and place a period on this conversation.

"Thanks, sweetheart," she breathed, sounding as if my consent lifted a burden from her.

"I am going to get ready to go. You okay?" I asked and searched her eyes for the truth.

Her eyes communicated great relief and peace. "Get a plate to take to home for Justin and my little man." She reached for me and kissed my forehead and said, "I love you with a love that knows no bounds, baby. Forgiveness can allow you to love that way too. Make sure you say goodbye to your Dad."

"I love you too, Mommy. I always will. Thanks for the food. I'll say goodbye to Aunt Dinah and then Karlie and I will be on our way. She is going to try to get on the road before dark." I placed my hand over hers. "Talk to you later this week."

As we walked to the car after saying our goodbyes, I told Karlie about Mom's eerie request.

"Maybe she wanted to share something with you that she feels is very important," she speculated.

"I kind of gathered that but it seemed really creepy, you know?"

"Stop reading into it, Paige and make sure you call your mom and most importantly, go and see her," she said with what I felt was an unwarranted reprimand.

"Alright, K. I hadn't planned on not touching base with Mom. Do you know something that I don't or should know?" I asked, beginning to feel a little bit overwhelmed by the subject matter.

"No, of course not. Do you think that she would disclose any family business that seems so sensitive to me and not to you first?" She seemed a little taken aback and her countenance changed to that of one who was just abruptly thrown a curve.

"I am sorry, K…It's…just…this seems so unlike Mom," I confessed. "She usually just told you the deal, then and there. There had never been a "wait till later" bone in her body.

"Don't sweat it, you'll know soon enough."

"I am so glad you made the trip to see me this weekend. Did you have fun?"

"I sure did, girl. Thanks for always making me feel so welcome."

We entered the house, thankful to be back and I gave K some time to get a quick nap so that she would feel rested enough to get on the road to head back home. I found a cute black skirt that had become too big for me and thought that it would look perfect on Karlie. I placed it on her suitcase. I love to send her home with something. I guess I inherited that from Mom. She always sent me home with an item of clothing, food or something for Justin and Adam. I am glad I have her kindness gene.

Later that night, after helping Justin get Adam to bed, I sat up in bed and worked on my presentation for a couple of hours.

"What are you reading?" Justin asked with a devilish smile.

"It's just a draft of a presentation that I had to complete for my meeting with VP's at Rosenfeld Data. Why?" I read the message nestled in his walnut colored eyes. His smirk told me that he wanted a little lovin'.

"Is Adam down for the count?" I asked. I was relieved that we had made up after our little misunderstanding.

He nodded as he slipped off his robe and kicked off his slippers, his seductive smile never left his handsome face.

"It was nice seeing Karlie. I just wish she could have brought Tyson and Tara with her," Justin said, climbing onto the bed and methodically removing the papers from my hands.

He smelled like he just took a shower. His breath was minty and fresh. Although a little preoccupied with thoughts of Mom, I tried to focus my attention on my husband. His lips were full and soft. It drove me crazy when his hands would be everywhere while his lips operated on mine. It was as if we were the only ones in the world. I wanted that feeling of freedom and reckless abandon to return to our lovemaking so desperately.

Whom the Son sets free, is free indeed...

I jumped almost imperceptibly but Justin noticed. His radar again...

The voice startled me and this time I recognized the words. They were from the bible. Who is talking to me?

Focus on your man, girl, I told myself.

"Are you okay?" he asked, kissing my neck. "I've missed you, Mrs. Covington," he whispered seductively as he began to kiss my ear and then continued to treat my neck to little pecks and bites.

"It's nice to be missed, Mr. Covington," I giggled and began to own his mouth as we reacquainted ourselves after our brief hiatus.

Chapter 8

I awoke with a start. I rolled over and looked over at the illuminated clock and found that it read 2:00 a.m. I couldn't remember my dream but knew that I didn't like where it was going and for some reason, I was able to take myself out it.

I decided to get up and check on Adam. I turned to see Justin sleeping on his back snoring loudly. Maybe his snoring is what knocked me out of the dream and not my own volition.

I slipped out of the bed, careful not to alert Justin's inner alarm. He stirred, mumbled something and rolled over.

Adam was also sleeping, a carbon copy of his father. Adam needed a sibling. I had forgotten to talk to Justin about an addition to the family. I'd talk to him about it once this thing with Mom was over.

Mom—what was up? I wondered.

She had been through a lot I am sure. I don't know why she put up with Dad all these years. I knew that it couldn't have been easy.

I recalled one pivotal day when my already decreasing respect and reverence for the leader of my church, Dad and God, really hit an all-time low.

The Young Adult Choir and the Youth Choir had just completed rehearsal and we heard loud talking and screaming coming from the lower level. We made our way out of the sanctuary and rushed toward to the conference area. We saw Deacon G. standing in front of the group of deacons, trustees and elders. He was very animated; arms flying and eyes bulging. We all stopped cold at the entrance and saw that Sis Hawks was standing as well. They were having a disagreement. A very bad disagreement. Our new pastor, the one who replaced Reverend Simon, Reverend Collier, was trying to achieve some type of order but to no avail.

"Pastor, you need to sit down because this has nothing to do with you!" she shouted without any thought about whom she was addressing or that she was in the house of the Lord.

"Sis Hawks, there isn't reason to—" Pastor Collier stated a little too tentatively.

"If you don't think his behavior needs to be addressed, then yes, I do think that there is a reason. If you can't act like a man or at least a man of God and keep your congregation from fraternizing with other congregations to spread gossip and acting like they haven't a church home, we haven't any use for you," she said in flurry of anger.

"Pastor, thank you but she is not acting appropriately and I will not continue this discussion while she is acting this way," Deacon G. said, regaining his composure.

"Deacon, thanks for using the sense God gave you. I mean that." He glared at Sis Hawks. "Sis Hawks, if you can't conduct yourself in a Christian fashion, you need to leave. Deacon Gerry is able to visit with other Christians and fellowship. Just because he attends a bible study led by another pastor of another church does not make him a Judas or anything like that. He has always thirsted for the Word. Whatever information provided to someone at Redeemed Baptist about your son and his sexual preferences when he was alive has nothing to do with it. I have every confidence that Deacon Gerry would not gossip about any such thing. You aren't even certain that it was Deacon Gerry that started this snowball of scandal, are you?"

Sister Hawks was barely audible when she said, "Well, no, but he should be more active in our own bible study." She remained standing determined to have her say.

As the drama played out, I was stunned. How could Sister Hawks behave this way? Before this happened, I had just started to observe her movements and behavior during service.

I noticed that every Sunday, like clockwork, on or about 12:20 p.m., she would begin her shouting fit. I never believed that she was glorifying God in any way but she had most of the church fooled. This happened when the pastor was revving up for his ending. The organist had reclaimed his seat at the organ and followed the minister's each phrase with a chord. At the culmination, Sister Hawks would begin to shout and slowly but skillfully make her way into the middle aisle for all to witness her fancy footwork. She could "cut a step" like no other in the congregation. If you didn't know it you'd think she was twenty-five and not sixty-three years of age.

"Deacon G is a very active member and—" Dad said and rose to his feet.

His involvement didn't surprise me because he always felt the need to interject something.

"Deacon Hunter, please don't let me get started on you," Sister Hawks said with a sinister snicker. "I am surprised that you are still a deacon here. We all know you helped Pastor Simon steal money from this church. Oh, and the way you do your lovely God-fearing wife is a shame before the Lord. I am sure that we all can share a story or two about you and your dealings," Sis Hawks stated with confidence and a smirk. Her look of vindication was sickening. She stared at Daddy, daring him to say another word.

Her statements, whether they were true or not, silenced Dad like the lions in the story of Daniel. He stood rooted to the spot as if her words paralyzed him.

"Sister Hawks, that is enough!" Pastor Collier shouted. It was clear that he had lost his composure.

"You are right, Pastor. I have said all that I wanted to say. I may not be perfect but there was never a day that I did anything that I was ashamed of," she said with note of superiority.

"Think again, Inez," a voice from the back of the room said. When the person stood up, all heads turned and we realized that it was my mom. Her eyes were on fire but her tone was controlled and her lips were tightened into a line. I didn't know how her words were escaping.

"You are here excreting your lies because your son died of AIDS and you know it was because he contracted it from another man. Face it, Inez, he was a homosexual. That news had somehow gotten out and your perfect little lie about your son crumbled as lies usually do. No one here condemned your son. We all prayed for his deliverance. We know that God didn't hate him, only the sin. We all have sinned. You know that. That's why we should thank God every day for Jesus." She stopped and looked around the room. "No one from the deacon board told anyone at Redeemed. Your mother told Pastor Chester at Redeemed. She is a member there. Did you think that maybe she asked for prayer from her own pastor?"

Sis Hawks looked dumfounded. "I told her not to say anything to anyone," she said, looking away as if remembering when she gave the instructions to her mother.

"As for me, I would rather not have your pity," Mom continued. "Sounding pious doesn't suit you, Inez. None of us, including yourself, have been saved all of our lives. In the future, please keep my personal life out of your conversations, in private or public."

With that said, my dad regained the use of his limbs and walked toward my mom.

"Stop, Evan. Not another step." Her hands were raised to emphasize her request. "Sis Hawks has done enough damage and has caused this church to waste too much time on an unnecessary issue."

My dad tried to inch closer to Mom. "I asked you not to come any further. There isn't a need. I will ask this of you for the sake of your family. Genuinely confess your sins and repent. I'll say no more." Her eyes were brimming with threatening tears. Instantly, her lips softened and the line disappeared. She grabbed her purse and bible. "Evan, the bible says 'For it had been better for them not to have known the way of righteousness, than, after they have known it, to turn from the holy commandment delivered unto them. 2nd Peter 5: 21."

I was stunned. My mother barely looked at me as she walked out of the room and up the stairs. Her head was held high. I heard the front doors of the church open and then close. It was all true. Wasn't it? Was Dad an adulterer and a thief? I felt my legs become jelly as the memory faded.

Chapter 9

"Are we all set to meet with the team at Rosenfeld on Thursday?" I asked the team during our prep conference call on Tuesday. I completed the Power Point presentation that outlined the new health reimbursement arrangement product. The team offered some feedback after my quick run-through. I decided to defer any questions regarding systemic limitations to our team lead as we had heard of some issues and I was not in the position nor did I feel comfortable with equivocating while in front of the client. It was a fact that some clients had experienced some issues as a result of system hiccups and I was confident that Myra could address those concerns if they came up.

There was silence and then a delayed, "I think we are ready" response from my teammates.

"If that is all, then we can close this call. We all know our roles for the meeting. It's important that we don't simply answer an inquiry if we are not one hundred percent confident and sure about the answer. I am told that they can sense indecision. If they pick up on any uncertainty, our credibility is shot before we even get started."

"Paige, what you have put together is just what we need to present to this type of client. Thankfully, you'll be doing much of the talking," Leeann, my counterpart stated. She was obviously very happy that she didn't have too much to say during the meeting.

"That's true but they may direct a certain question, such as the rate comparisons and network discounts, to you guys. I haven't too much exposure to those aspects and will need you guys to be ready to jump in," I stated, certain that because Rosenfeld was bottom-line oriented, the topic would be broached.

"You are right, Paige," Myra agreed. "Leeann, let's touch base with the underwriter about that so that our information is solid."

"I am on it," Leeann confirmed.

"Okay, team, we are done. Thanks for joining the call. Oh, one more thing, Kate, as implementation lead, could you please ensure that you note any meeting take-aways so that we can de-brief and get answers to the client by Tuesday of next week? Let's schedule to de-brief on Friday. If you could send out invites to all that would be great," I said.

"Sure, that's no problem, Paige," Kate agreed.

"Everyone have a good day. We'll see you on Thursday, at 9:45 a.m. in the client's lobby."

As I closed the lid to my laptop, I checked the time. Yesterday and today flew by. It was already 4:23 p.m. My back was stiff and I was tired. I silently recounted my day and remembered that I needed to have the hard copy of the presentation sent to me. I re-opened my laptop and e-mailed my administrative assistant to print out the presentation and have it overnighted. She responded positively almost immediately. "I love you, Kia," I responded via e-mail. Almost immediately after I clicked send, the phone rang..

"I love you too, Paige," Kia sang. I could hear her smiling through the phone.

"You are always there when I need you, girl," I laughed, letting my professional guard down to talk with my "sister."

"I just want to be blessing to anyone I can," she said nonchalantly. "Oops, I am sorry, Paige, I don't want to force my spirituality on you but I know that you'll get revelation soon. I've been praying for you," she revealed.

"I don't mind you being a blessing to me, Kia, and prayers won't hurt either especially since I am going in front of the Rosenfeld people on Thursday."

Kia laughed. "I am glad to hear that, from what I hear, you are going to need some providential intervention for that meeting. They are tough."

"I don't desire to nor can I get into Jesus right now. I just can't deal—"

"Paige, you seem to have some knowledge of Jesus Christ based on our conversations in the past. I just get the feeling that you are distancing yourself from Him because of things that have nothing to do with Him," Kia said with a concerned and serious tone.

"Kia, it had everything to do with Him. You wouldn't believe the things that I have seen and experienced and all in the name of Christ or under the guise of Christianity."

"I won't belabor the point. You'll have to make the decision for yourself. Please, my sistah, don't wait too long. I am not giving up on you, girl." Her happy go-lucky voice returned. "The binders will get to your house tomorrow by 12:00 p.m. Have a **blessed** evening," she stressed the word blessed and chuckled.

"Bye, Kia and thanks for your help."

After dinner, I decided that I had better call Mom to set up a time to talk.

"Are you still unnerved about what your mom wanted to talk to you about?" Justin asked after putting away the crock-pot. He sometimes helped me wash the dishes when I cooked dinner. He was in a good mood because I made pot roast in the crock-pot. He was right, cooking it all day made it much more tender than the way I usually cooked it. It was seasoned to perfection and the gravy was just the way he liked it. Adam even had a couple nice things to say about it and he wasn't a fan of pot roast. The mashed potatoes were his favorite part of the meal. To make everyone happy, I decided that since Adam liked peas, they would be the vegetable for the night. Both of my men were happy.

"Yes, I guess I am a bit apprehensive about calling her. She sounded like she had done us a disservice by being our mother. I think that she was wonderful mother."

I recounted the conversation. He smiled at the comment Mom

made about finding a good husband but he was perplexed about the whole "mother" aspect.

"I guess you'll have to sit down with her and talk it all out. Are you going to go with your sisters?"

"Nope, she mentioned that she saw the need to pray for me more than Celia, Loni and Darlene. What does that mean? Am I some sort of bad seed?" I asked.

"No, babe. I don't think that is what she meant," he said, walking over to me and placing his arms around me. "Bad seed, you? Not a chance, Miss Goody-Two-Shoes."

I pushed him away and we both laughed.

"What is so funny?" Adam asked, looking at both of us.

"Your daddy was making fun of me," I whined making a sad face and exaggerating a pout.

"Daddy, you shouldn't be mean to Mom," Adam said, fists up as he tried to defend me.

"I am sorry, Mom," Justin said contritely.

"That is better. You apology is accepted." I looked at Adam and winked.

The phone began to ring and Adam answered it.

"Hi. Grandpa!" Adam exclaimed. "Thanks for the Transformer."

There was a pause and Adam slowly turned to me and handed me the phone. I apprehensively took it from him. I didn't want to talk to Dad but something told me that wasn't why I didn't want to take the phone.

"Paige, your mom's pressure has been dangerously high since this afternoon. She collapsed while making dinner. We are at the hospital and I think that you need to get here as soon as you can."

I stood stunned for a moment and heard myself say that I was on my way. The sound of the handset of the phone hitting the floor caused Justin to turn to face me. I hadn't realized that I dropped it. His eyes seemed to read mine and all at once he grabbed his keys and we left for the hospital.

Chapter 10

We arrived at the hospital and saw Loni standing at the entrance, pacing. She was visibly upset and that only aided in the augmenting my feelings of anxiety and fear. I grabbed Justin's hand to steady myself and he gave it a quick squeeze before we reached Loni. I didn't dare look at him because I knew that I would begin crying. I certainly didn't need to lose it prior to even seeing Mom.

Dad's voice sounded so weird on the phone. I never heard him sound that way before. I heard his voice crack and the deep and resounding confidence that he exuded even when he was dead-wrong was absent.

"Loni, what's going on? How is Mom?" I asked. My words seemed to quickly empty into the air.

"Her blood pressure was so elevated that she passed out. She has not regained consciousness. It happened about 2:00 p.m. this afternoon and she hasn't moved her lips or said anything since she was admitted. Dad says that she was coming down the stairs after cleaning the bathroom. It seems that she was about to put dinner on but lost her footing and almost tumbled down the stairs. Thankfully he was there to catch her. She complained about being dizzy." Loni stopped to take a breath and took a drag. She seemed really shaken. I really wished she didn't smoke.

"Dad said that he sat her down on the couch to allow her to regain her equilibrium but her eyes began to roll back into her head and she began speaking inaudibly and slurring her words. Then she collapsed."

Recounting the story that she received from Dad apparently caused Loni to become more upset.

"What are we going to do, Paige?" She began to cry. As I released Justin's hand to go to Loni, I realized that I had a vise grip on his hand. Out of the corner of my eye I saw him wiggle them to allow circulation. I smiled at him in a weak effort to apologize. He shook his head no as if to say, "Don't worry about it." He nodded toward Loni. I focused my attention on her again and placed my arms around her. She was trembling.

"Mom is strong. She is going to come through this." I said this but was not completely sure that I believed what I was saying. I knew Mom was a survivor. Anyone who knew Mom would say that but this was different. Were her mind and body simply tired of the drama and neglect that she received throughout the years? She took care of herself but certain health issues kept rearing their ugly heads. Her blood pressure was a constant culprit.

"How do you know, Paige?" Loni said almost angrily. "What makes you so sure that she will come out of it and if she does, will she be the same?" She looked at me with so much anger that I had to turn away. I knew that it was displaced but that fact didn't make me feel any better. I looked at Justin, unable to respond to her question. I wanted to tell her that I didn't know but we had to believe that the God that Mom worshiped would bring her through. I didn't have any confidence in God but she always did and that was all that mattered. Wasn't it?

The payers of the righteous availeth much.

The words caressed my trembling heart as they found a resting place in my mind.

"Paige is right, Loni. Your mom is a trooper. She knows that we are here for her," Justin said as he apprehensively took Loni's hand. Feeling a little stronger together, we all walked into the hospital to find Mom's room.

When approaching the room, I heard Dad's voice. I would have stopped and waited for him to leave the area before entering the space but my mom was in that hospital bed and all I could think of was getting to her. I needed to place my hands on her face to know that she was still with us. I walked right up to the bed, past Dad, Celia and Blue, Celia's husband, and placed my hand on Mom's face to feel her warmth. I breathed a sigh of temporary relief.

I looked back and noticed that everyone was staring at me.

"What is the doctor saying?" I asked, addressing no one in particular.

Dad was sitting in the chair right next to where I was standing, just holding Mom's hand. His eyes were red and his faced looked gaunt. He looked like he had aged since Sunday.

"They are trying to reduce her pressure with medication but she has not opened her eyes. They said that her body simply gave out," Celia said. Blue was holding her protectively. Celia was not able to handle a lot of stress. Mom was right when she said we picked the right men. Blue was good for Celia. He was a large man with coal-colored skin. Blue had an incredibly peaceful demeanor that put you immediately at ease. I looked at my loving husband and he opened his arms and I walked to him and let him hold me as well. I reached over to Loni to hold her had, knowing that Tyler, her husband, was on his way. Darlene was out of the country and trying to get the first flight back. I hoped that she was okay. It had to be a horrible feeling knowing that you were so far away from home and family when a crisis hits. We needed each other. All of us needed to be strong for each other.

Suddenly, while standing with Justin and looking at Mom, I recalled what Loni said about Mom cleaning the bathroom. Cleaning the bathroom? My mind provided a visual of Mom tired from cleaning the bathroom, standing at the kitchen counter beginning to make dinner for Dad. Anger began to rise in me like a bubbling volcano, preparing for an eruption. My eyes found the back of my dad's head and I almost exploded. I wanted to scream at my dad. Steadying myself while walking toward my father, the words that I released were dripping with accusation.

"If you knew that her pressure was dangerously high, what in the world was she doing cleaning a bathroom and cooking dinner when you were there and could have cleaned and made a simple meal for her?" Justin grabbed my hand as if to tell me to stop. I looked back at him and his eyes silenced me. I closed my mouth with force, knowing that Justin was right. I wanted to add, "After all these years and all of the things that you have caused her to endure, you couldn't have washed your own toilet?" I didn't allow those words into the atmosphere. Tears began to fill my eyes and although the water distorted my vision, my mind kept going. I silently promised my dad that there was not a reason in the world that would absolve him of this.

My father stood and turned slowly to look at me. I returned his look with my own icy stare. His eyes displayed the hurt that I wanted to inflict. I didn't have to say all of the things that I wanted to say. He knew exactly how I felt.

Good, I thought.

He tried to leave but I cut him off at the door. "No, Deac," I said sarcastically, "you stay and pray to the God you have been so faithful to. I know He'll hear *your* prayers."

I looked at my sisters, Justin and Blue apologetically. I was sorry that they had to witness my temper but I couldn't stop myself.

"I am sorry, guys." I walked out the room to find a place to call Ms. Debbie to check on Adam.

Sitting in a chair in the family lounge area, eyes closed, I began think about the words that I hurled at my father. I rationalized my behavior by telling myself that it was long overdue but something inside of me told me that it was the wrong place and the wrong time to call him on the carpet. That is not to say that it wouldn't have happened eventually, but the hurt that I saw in his eyes was hard to shake. Celia and Loni were visibly taken aback by my controlled yet lethal outburst but I appreciated them just allowing me to say what I needed to say. I knew that it was utterly disrespectful but hadn't he done his share of disrespecting us?

"You okay?" I opened my eyes and saw Justin standing in front of me. He still had the look of concern but a little smirk was teasing the corners of his mouth.

"I will be once Mom regains consciousness," I said, while entwining his fingers in mine.

"Don't you think you were a little rough on the old man? I mean, based on what you said he was a trip but this was not exactly the right time to read him the riot act," he said.

I nodded in agreement. "I don't know what happened. One moment I was thinking that we needed to be strong for each other and the next minute, I was thinking of her scrubbing a toilet when she wasn't well." I felt the sting of tears but refused to release them. "Why should I be easy on him? He sure wasn't easy on her." My anger began to fuel itself again. I was determined not to let it control me.

"I have got to leave a message for June to let her know that I will not be available tomorrow via e-mail but will be checking my v-mail. I still have to plan to go the Rosenfeld meeting on Thursday but—"

"Don't worry about doing that just now. You can certainly call her in the morning," Justin said. "For now, as long as we know that Ms. Debbie can watch Adam for a couple more hours, let's just go back to your mom's room to get an update, okay."

Justin pulled me to my feet and kissed my forehead. "You have to promise me on behalf of your mother that there won't be any more discord. You know she wouldn't like that," he warned.

"I promise and thanks for understanding me so well." I gave him a quick peck on his lips and we headed back to the room. I was determined to keep my promise. At least for now.

I noticed Dr. Jamison standing outside of Mom's hospital room as Justin and I turned the corner exiting the lounge. He was nodding his head while Dad was speaking to him. I began to quicken my steps, pulling Justin along to find out what was being discussed.

"Her pressure has stabilized. It is not where we would like it but it is closer to the goal and much lower than it was. We are certainly happy to report that, Mr. Hunter." After all of the years he has known our family and has treated us, he still remained formal.

"Is she out of the woods?" I asked, finally reaching the conferring men. My heart was in my throat as I waited for a response.

"Hello, Paige," Dr. Jamison said. "She is not out of danger but as I was telling your father, her pressure has decreased and she has to remain in bed and she must rest. She shouldn't get out of bed to perform any other task than to relieve herself. I know Mrs. Hunter and she can be very, shall I say, independent and strong-willed. You must let her know that she has to take it easy for own good." He looked at me and then his gaze settled on Dad.

"I am assuming that she has regained consciousness," I said.

"No, Paige, she has not," Dr. Jamison said. "That is what has me confused. We were pretty sure that the cause was her blood pressure but apparently there is something else going on. We have run tests and there doesn't seem to be anything physically wrong other than the elevated pressure. We are confident that she will regain consciousness and wanted provide direction prior to her awakening to ensure that we are all on the same page." He placed his cocoa-colored hands into his pocket and leaned against the wall. "Why don't you go in and talk to her, Paige? I think that the voices of her loved ones may help. We will be certain to keep you posted should we find anything that may be causing this delay in her regaining consciousness." With that, he shook Dad's hand and placed his hand on my shoulder.

"Thanks, Dr. Jamison," Dad said.

He nodded, acknowledging our gratitude and walked down the hallway.

I quickly walked into the room and looked at Mom. All of the tubes had been removed except for one that was attached somehow into her hand. I walked over to the side of her bed and gazed at her face. Mom looked tired but strangely at peace. "Don't get too peaceful, Mom, I still need you," I whispered into her ear.

I turned to see Justin enter the room with Dad.

"I don't understand," I breathed, feeling confused while looking at Justin. "Why doesn't she wake up?"

"I don't know, baby." He looked as confused and concerned as I probably sounded. My back was to Mom and he continued to watch at her. "Wait. Look," he said and pointed in the direction of Mom's bed.

I quickly turned to see that her lips were moving but there wasn't anything being said. This was weird.

"Dad!" I said almost screaming. "Look!"

Dad moved closer and stood at the other side of Mom's bed. Her lips continued to move.

"I am here, Livie. I am here. I need you to come back to me. I need you so much." Droplets of water began to fall from Dad's eyes onto his hands as he held onto Mom. I was unable to stay in the room and turned to leave.

"Don't leave, Paige, I need you here too," Dad said. I was shocked by his words and decided to stay for just a moment. We stood there for about fifteen minutes. All the while, Mom continued to speak noiselessly.

Celia and Loni rushed in and informed us that Darlene's plane had just landed. They were amazed to see Mom talking and it soon registered that nothing was coming out her mouth. I directed them subtly out of the room and updated them on what had been going on.

Upon reentering the room, Celia and Loni observed Mom in a state bewilderment. Mouth agape, Celia walked closer to Mom's bed and whispered, "This is a first."

We all laughed knowing how true that statement was. It was a timely observation. We needed some levity and were clearly thankful that Mom was showing signs of improvement even if she wasn't conscious.

"Mom," I said leaning over the railing, "I have to go get your beautiful grandson home to bed. I am glad to know that you are doing a little better and I'll be back to see you in the morning. I love you, Mom." I kissed her on her forehead.

"Tell Darlene I'll see her tomorrow," I said to Celia and Loni.

I connected visually with each one in the room. "Please call me with any news. Don't wait until the morning. Promise?"

"We promise," Celia and Loni said in unison. Blue simply nodded and Tyler looked at Loni as if to say it was her call.

"I'll be here for most of the night, I will call each of you if anything changes," Dad confirmed.

"Thanks. Goodnight," I said as I exhaled, clearly needing to get home.

"When you come back tomorrow, I think we need to talk," Dad said as the countenance that I recognized emerged.

"Yes, I would agree," I responded impassively. Feeling exhausted, Justin and I headed toward the exit.

Trying to explain Adam why his grandmother was is in the hospital proved to be a little less difficult that we anticipated. We were sure that he wouldn't understand the blood pressure aspect, so we simply decided to tell him that her body was not working the way that it should and it caused her to sleep without her really thinking that she was tired.

"It's almost like when I tell you that you need to take a nap because I can tell that you are tired and need the rest. Sometimes you don't agree and think that you can stay up the entire day, but because I know you, I make you take a nap so that you won't get sick or get yourself in trouble."

Adam nodded. "Sometimes I don't like to take a nap," he agreed.

"Well that is what happened with Grandma, she wasn't listening to her body. She needed to take it easy because her body was sending her messages that it needed help and rest but she kept going and didn't rest."

"Now it is forcing her to get the help that she needs," Justin added as he picked up Adam and placed him on his knee.

"I understand now." Looking at both of us, he asked, "How long will she be sleeping? When will she get up? Sometimes it's not good to sleep too long."

"Well, she will sleep until her body tells her to wake up," I guesstimated. I was unsure as to how to respond to that question and didn't want to lie.

"I think Mom is right. Your body just wakes you up when your nap is over, right?" Justin asked Adam.

"Uh-huh," Adam said.

"Although the situation is not exactly the same, we are hopeful that the same thing will happen," Justin said. "Now it's time to get you to bed, little man."

He picked up Adam and playfully plopped him on his bed.

Adam pushed away his comforter and retreated from the bed with a serious look on his face. I almost wanted to laugh because he seemed so resolute. "Mom, Dad, I know that you don't pray to God, but can I say a prayer to God to help Grandma's body get the rest it needs so that she can wake up? Grandma is always saying that God can heal the sick. She is sick now and because she is a child of God, I know He will heal her if we ask."

Suffer the little children to come unto Me and forbid them not; for such is the kingdom of God.

He smiled with such confidence that I reached out and hugged him, restraining tears.

I was somewhat taken aback by what I heard. The voice confirmed that I should let my son pray for his grandmother.

Before I could answer Adam's request, Justin knelt on the floor with Adam and grabbed my hand to join them. "I think that it is a good idea," Justin said.

Adam prayed for God to heal Mom's body in the name of Jesus Christ with such assurance that I all I could do was nod my head and squeeze Justin's hand. I couldn't exactly explain what I was feeling once Adam finished praying for everyone in our family, so I decided that an explanation wasn't necessary and swept it to the back of my mind.

"Mom, Grandma is going to be okay," Adam confided. He kissed Justin and then me.

"Good night, sweet baby. Daddy will put out the light," I said. I was so proud of him. Why was I so proud? I didn't pray to God, so why was I happy that my son was? As I walked away from Adam's room, I heard Justin telling him that he was very proud of him and that the prayer was definitely going to help Grandma. I had absolutely nothing to say because I didn't want to hinder the prayer that was sent to God from my child, a true believer. I used to be one.

Chapter 11

"June, she has not regained consciousness so I will be at the hospital for the duration of the day today." I was not concerned about any problems that my boss might have had with my not having e-mail access today. My mom was in the hospital.

"I still plan to attend the meeting tomorrow at Rosenfeld Data but as soon as my part of the presentation is over, I will be getting on the road. We had a prep call earlier this week so we should be all set."

June, my boss, was a company woman. I think that she'd sell her first-born if it meant moving up in the organization. I really didn't want to have a long conversation about my familial issues just to have the details sent around the company. I tried to keep the dialogue to a minimum but she seemed to be concerned about the upcoming meeting with Rosenfeld.

"I am sure that at everything is in place and remember this is only a sample presentation that outlines the new product. The client may or may not want to use it. I'll call you from the road after the meeting. I must go now but feel free to leave a message on my v-mail. I'll be checking it every hour unless something changes with my mother. Thanks for your concern." I quickly ended the call so that I could get Adam off to camp. Justin decided to go in to work after making me promise to call with any news. I saw no reason for Adam to miss his trip to the skating rink with the rest of the kids from camp and decided that he should go about his normal activities as well.

When I re-entered the kitchen, Adam had just finished his cereal. He devoured my Cap'n Crunch. He and I both loved that sugary sweet cereal.

"You ready, baby?" I asked.

"Yes, Mom. Are you going to the hospital?" he asked as he downed the rest of his orange juice.

"Yes, I plan to go after the gym. I thought I'd take a step class this morning. I need to release some stress. I am kind of wound up because I am worried about Grandma," I explained.

"Grandma, always said not to worry. She said to tell Jesus about the problem and let him handle it. Worrying doesn't help," he said, placing the empty bowl into the sink as instructed.

I smiled at him and thought, *Who is this child?*

"You are right, baby. Let's go."

While driving to hospital, my cell phone rang and I put in my ear plugs so that I could speak hands-free.

"Hi, sweetie," Karlie greeted. "How are you doing this morning? I decided against calling you last night knowing that you needed some time with your family after the crazy evening that you must have had. I spent the time praying for you and your mom. Paige, she is going to be okay."

"Well you, Justin and Adam are definitely on the same page," I said. I told her about Adam and his prayer request as well as his certainty that Mom was going tot be fine.

"And a little child shall lead them…" She laughed. "Paige, you are being surrounded by His people. I find it hard to believe that nothing has made an impact. Just because you choose not to hear Him, does not mean that He is not speaking to your heart. Don't continue to harden your heart."

"Karlie, it's funny that you mentioned that because I have been hearing words come to me but the voice is not perceptible. The words communicate things that I seem to already know. It's weird, you know?" I paused and allowed myself to breathe. "I guess I just don't want to mentally recognize it." I didn't understand why I was able to admit my stubbornness aloud to Karlie but was unable to act on the voice that I had heard. It was the same voice each time I heard it. "I know it doesn't make any sense. My mother told me about the Holy Spirit or the inner witness but I have been so far removed from God that I don't think that it could be that. Could it?" I began to get flustered and as a result, my voice became animated. Calm tried to return when I reached the hospital and parked my car.

"Paige, do me a favor, the next time you hear it, call me. Okay? I believe that there is hope for you yet," Karlie said and began to hum with a little too much mirth.

"Wait. I don't know if I want to talk to God or have Him talk to me. If He has been talking to me, then why do I continue to feel so unsure, lost and confused?" I almost yelled. Fear and indecision gripped me as I recalled how people had claimed to have the spirit communicate with them and even lead them. They were later found out to be liars and hypocrites. "I don't want anything false. I need assurance. Last night my baby had such confidence. He knew the truth when he prayed for Mom last night. I am tired of hypocrisy and that is why I have stayed away from Christ. If I talk to God or if He chooses to speak to me, I want it to be real."

"Paige, I don't have all of the answers nor can I explain why you had to witness so much religious duplicity in your life but it is not our purpose to understand all of the mysteries of the world but simply to trust that God loves us and knows what is best for us. We should trust God with a child's simplicity and purity."

I inhaled. Uneasiness and confusion lay siege to my mind and heart.

"Easier said than done, Karlie. Talk to you later."

Chapter 12

I entered the hospital and stopped at the nurses' station. I asked for the head nurse, introduced myself and inquired about Mom's condition. I quickly read her name tag and saw that her name was Anne Modestte.

"She is resting right now. We are keeping close watch on her as she still hasn't regained consciousness but the lip movement hasn't stopped. Her pressure is on the high end of normal but that is not our main concern. Your father is in the room now trying to talk to her. I don't think that he has been very successful but we continue to hope that she'll awaken soon."

"Thanks, Ms. Modestte. I think I'll go in and sit with Mom for a little while," I responded, disappointed that Mom's situation had not improved during the night.

"No thanks is necessary, Mrs. Covington. I have had the opportunity to speak with Mrs. Hunter on many occasions. She has frequently visited people in this hospital. She has a comforting spirit and is true child of God. I count it a privilege to offer any help that I can. I will continue to pray for her recovery. Oh, and please call me Anne." Ms. Modestte smiled warmly and touched my hand.

"Your kindness is appreciated," I said. "I'll stop by the desk before leaving." Anxious to get to Mom, I turned and walked into the room.

Mom seemed unmoved from the position that we left her in last night. As I walked closer to her bed, Dad turned toward me. I nodded my greeting and placed my hand on hers and kissed her forehead. "Hi, Mom," I whispered into her ear. She looked as if she were sleeping. Her skin was so flawless and beautiful. I couldn't see any wrinkles. "I would really appreciate it if you would come back to us. We need to hear your voice. You'd be so proud of your grandson. He prayed for you last night. You would have...uhm...both of you would have been proud."

I looked up at Dad to include him into the conversation. Dad's eyes were dark. "Why don't you go and get something for lunch? I'll stay with Mom until you get back."

"I am not that hungry. I think that you and I need to talk. It is no secret that you have less than fond feelings for me and I can't say that I don't understand because I do, but you need to understand something..."

"Dad, let's not get into that right now. I would really like to focus on Mom. I think that she needs all of the positive energy that we can muster. Talking right now will not be a positive exchange and I don't want to go there with you."

I looked down at Mom before I began to speak again and her lips began to move. The heart monitor made a loud noise and I jumped. "Dad, get the nurse," I said hurriedly. "Get Nurse Anne!"

Nurse Anne rushed in and read the monitor. Alarm registered on her face. "You both must leave the room. Her pressure has elevated again."

Nurse Anne pressed a button on the wall and almost immediately two nurses and a man, the resident physician, entered the room. They lowered the railings and began to further examine Mom.

"You will have to leave," Nurse Anne said again. Her eyes were without emotion but her voice was firm.

Confused and scared, I reluctantly left the room and stood outside the door. The sounds of machines beeping and whirring began to make me dizzy. A few feet to my left, I saw a chair so I made my way to the chair and sat down. Dad wasn't far behind me.

"What is going on? Do you think that we upset her?" I considered as Dad grabbed the other chair and sat down.

"She has been upset with me regarding you and I for some time," he revealed, seeming remorseful. "If I could change some of the bad choices that I have made in my life, I would. Paige, I can't change them and now I am going to lose the only woman who truly loved me, for me. She stood by me when no one else would or even could." He stood and looked down the hall. "God, please don't take her from me. She is all I ever wanted." It seemed as if he wasn't even cognizant of my presence. He began to pray to God. I couldn't understand what he was saying and decided that I couldn't just sit there any longer. I had to get up to find out what was going on. As I peered into the room, I noticed that the beeping had stopped and Nurse Anne was the only one left in the room. She saw me and motioned that I could enter.

"We have once again stabilized her but we are not sure how long she will remain that way," she conveyed.

"Can anyone tell us what is going with her? Why is she moving her lips but not talking? We were of the understanding that because her pressure decreased, she would wake up but she hasn't. What are going to be the next steps? Someone needs to tell us something. This is all becoming too much." I knew I was rambling and Nurse Anne's expression confirmed it as her eyes held mine with solemn understanding. It was as if I couldn't dam the words and the questions tumbling out of my mouth.

"Mrs. Covington, we honestly don't know why your mother's condition has not changed after her pressure began to decrease. That seems to be puzzling Dr. Jamison as well as his colleagues." She walked over to me and said, "Personally, I am holding fast to the belief that God knows what He is doing and that she will awaken soon."

I stared at my mother. The lip movement had ceased and she was now in a peaceful slumber. "I don't know how much of this I can take," I said, exhausted.

The large round black and white clock that hung like the moon over the nurses' station told me that it was 3:00 p.m. I had to get home and get ready for my meeting with Rosenfeld in the morning. The trip was about two hours. Because of the distance, I planned to leave that night to be fresh and alert for the 10:00 a.m. meeting.

I kissed Mom's forehead and said goodbye. I wasn't even sure that she heard me but I hoped that she did. I thanked Nurse Anne for her help and gave her my cell phone number. I asked that she or someone from her staff call me if there were any changes in Mom's conditn. She said that she would. I was grateful that she knew Mom and that she would look out for her.

I turned to walk to the elevator, deciding to go to the cafeteria to search for Dad. Just as I was about to board the elevator, I saw him walking in my direction. I walked down the corridor to meet him halfway.

"Dad, I am leaving. I have to go out of town but you have all of my numbers if you need anything or if you need to contact me." I tried not to look at him but he grabbed my hand while I was speaking.

"Paige, you must hear me out. I am not concerned about what you'll think of me because it can't be any worse than what I've thought of myself but there are things that you must know," he said, almost pleading. "Your mother has long since forgiven me and you and your sisters' forgiveness is what I need."

"Dad, we'll talk when I get back," I said evasively. I really didn't want to talk to him about how he had only been a fake and a phony and how time and time again he had caused heartache and embarrassment. Why did God even allow him to sit in anybody's church? Did God stop caring that he and countless others went around acting so pious but cheated, stole and lied? Had He stopped convicting people's hearts to do the right thing? Why did I even care anymore? I shook my head slightly. My mother, the most caring, kind and loving person I knew, was sick. Dad, who was the total opposite, was standing before me in perfectly good health and had the audacity to spout this nonsense. Incredulous, I looked past him, not trusting myself to actually make visual contact.

"I have to pack for a business trip and won't be back until tomorrow evening," I said. I really wanted to say, "To be totally honest, I don't think that I want to hear what you have to say," Instead, I said, "When Mom regains consciousness, we'll talk."

"Paige, I am not sure that she will and she wanted me to talk to you if she didn't get the opportunity," he responded.

"What? How would you know that?" I asked angrily. He would try anything to get me to hear his sorry excuses.

"She wanted to me to talk to you and I want to keep my promise," he repeated.

"Alright," I said sarcastically, "I'll come by the hospital when I get back in town tomorrow evening." I didn't believe him but what did I have to loose? "I'll be back around 4:00 p.m. I'll talk to you then."

"Paige, thank you," he said as I walked onto the elevator.

I nodded as the doors closed.

Chapter 13

"Although we like the information that has been presented, Paige, and needless to say we want you to present the information at each of our locations, how can we ensure that our employees will take an interest in this new benefit option?" Carl asked. His face was impassive as he posed the question.

I quickly looked at my team to let them know that I would respond to the question. Carl was the vice president of human resources and the one that we had to please.

"Carl, we can certainly create a communications calendar that will ensure not only that Rosenfeld employees understand the plan but give them insight into the product. We will use examples similar to the ones outlined in the presentation. We can also emphasize the significant cost savings which will undoubtedly make it more appealing. Rosenfeld can certainly assist us in this endeavor by possibly making the cost for this particular product one of the less expensive offerings since you plan to keep the HMO plan in place. We have found that a number of our customers have used this strategy and it has been most successful in shifting the population." Hoping that I had answered his question, I punted the question to Myra to allow her to close it out. "Myra, I am sure, can assist you with that aspect. I can work with your team with regard to the communications."

Myra nodded emphatically and added, "I certainly can work some numbers and schedule a call including the underwriter to make certain that we achieve the membership numbers that you are shooting for."

Walking to my seat, I decided that I needed to interject that once they signed off on the presentation that would be used, and we made the requested tweaks, each location would receive a copy. Because there might be instances when I would not able to attend the enrollment meeting, a counterpart who resided in that area would have the information and the presentation. He or she would be able to facilitate the meetings. I informed them that that was one of perks of doing business with a national insurance company.

Leann smiled. She knew that I didn't plan on traipsing across the country when there was someone local who could simply cover the meeting for me. She and I had talked about this and promised that we'd back each other up when that issue was presented.

Kate had a few questions to ask Carl and his team. Liza, Rosenfeld's benefits manager, didn't have the answers but promised that she'd get back to Kate next week. Myra and Leann really didn't have too much to incorporate into the dialogue. I guessed Myra was right, it was certainly my show. As for me, the meeting was over. I was skillfully able to respond to the inquiries posed by the Rosenfeld team. My job now was simply to wait for them to get back to me with their changes once they reviewed the updated presentation. There were a few items that they took issue with but those were relatively minor. The change of font and removal of color, could be easily remedied. I didn't know how we were going to ensure that the physicians would be up to speed on this new product because Rosenfeld was concerned about the doctors and their staff not knowing how to bill the insurance company. I'd have to work with the provider relations department to draft some sort of letter to put in the client packets to highlight that the physicians in the client's specific area were aware of the product and its nuances.

Standing in a huddle in the parking lot, we quickly discussed the meeting. I really thought that this review could wait. It was 12:45 p.m. and I wanted to get on the road.

"The presentation was fabulous, Paige. The client really thought it touched on the important aspects of the HRA plan. I know that their requested changes were unusual, but let's get them completed and submitted to them as soon as we can," Myra said.

"That shouldn't be a problem. There were minor things. I am going to need your influence when talking with provider relations. They may be reluctant to create correspondence for a single client when it really isn't going to impact network use," I warned her.

"No worries. That'll be mine," Myra stated.

"Kate, Leann, are you okay with the things that you need to handle?" I asked as I picked up my binder and briefcase.

They both nodded affirmatively. "Don't forget to send the invite for the detailed de-brief for next week." I looked at Leann hoping that she would remember to get it done. Although we originally wanted to debrief tomorrow, it was agreed that we would wait until early next week. Kate was good but she had a lot of accounts to implement and Rosenfeld might not be a priority because it was an existing account. New accounts were always the priority. Silently asking Leann to ensure that we had the call scheduled was a way of providing the needed deliverables.

"I am out of here," I announced. "Safe travels to you guys."

"You don't want to go to lunch?" Myra asked.

"No, I really have to get back," I said declining while simulating reluctance. I saw no need to explain to them that my mom was in the hospital because it would be all over the department by the evening.

"Thanks anyway. I'll let you treat me on the next trip," I said to Myra with a practiced smile. "Talk to you guys next week, if not sooner."

With that, I walked over to my rental car and placed the binder and briefcase into the back seat and started the engine. I was glad that client meeting was over. As I played the morning back in my mind, I mentally paused at the point when Myra performed the introductions at the onset of the meeting. I don't think that Rosenfeld expected me to be African-American. Their faces clearly revealed their surprise when I was introduced. This seemed to be becoming the norm.

I'd like to know what they expected. I don't think there was anything different about the way I spoke. Correct English is correct English. It really shouldn't be owned or used by a sole race. Oh well. Surprise! I am Black! When I attempted to achieve eye contact when presenting material, each of the Rosenfeld attendees, especially Carl, averted my gaze. I found that unusual. It was disturbing because I was always told that I should be wary of anyone who couldn't look you in the eye. They seemed taken aback when I confidently responded to their questions and not Myra. Now that I think about it, Myra seemed a little ill at ease with that as well. It was not my intention to take over but it was decided that I would lead the meeting. I had always been told that Myra was not to be trusted. I would continue to be on the look-out for any suspicious behavior from her.

Chapter 14

Driving home I decided that I would try and prepare myself for the conversation that Dad and I were going to have. I wasn't looking forward to it but I had a number of questions that required explanations. What made him think that he could be so easily forgiven for all of the horrible things that he had done to Mom, not to mention me, my sisters and others. He had obviously lied, cheated and stolen. How could he sit in that front pew every Sunday morning and claim to be a child of God and conduct his life so unlike Christ? I guess that he was in good company. A number of the members of my old church behaved the same way and seemed to dare you to call them on it. Infidelity and backbiting seemed to be the order of the day. What would possess someone to get up from their mistress's bed, take a shower and step into church singing, "Oh, how I love Jesus" all the way to their seat? My biggest question was where was God when all of this was taking place? How could He allow the desecration of His name? Just then it hit me, I was angry with God for allowing all of things that I witnessed. Yes, that was exactly it. My fist began to hit the steering wheel as the realization began to wash over me like cold water. The people that I witnessed cursing at each other and calling one another everything but a child of God were the same ones passing out the collection plate or a gospel tract. God had allowed them to turn His house into a charade and I had been angry with God all of these years. Why did He allow such things to transpire in His name? "That is why I don't want to have anything to do with You!" I screamed into the air. "I believed in You and You continued to disappoint me. You said that You remove every unclean thing but You didn't. How can I trust You? Why should I even believe in You anymore?" I began to feel a little warm and decided to increase the air conditioning. I noticed that my grip on the wheel was unyielding and although tears refused to drop from my eyes, they had reddened. "Could it be that the absence of You as active part of my life has caused me to feel the way I have been feeling for so long?" I asked Him. Nothing seemed to make sense. I blinked and stared straight ahead, determined not to get emotional.

"Forget it," I said aloud recognizing that my exit from the highway was next.

Having made known unto us the mystery of His will, according to **His good pleasure** *which he has purposed himself. Paige, my ways are not your ways…*

Although I completely and clearly heard the voice, I didn't want to hear that God would reveal His plan when I listened to Him and obeyed.

Because I encountered a lot of traffic on my way back, I decided that I'd go straight to the hospital and not go home first as initially planned. I wanted to get this conversation with Dad over with. With about thirty minutes of driving to go, I decided to eject my audio book, *Dark Corner,* by Brandon Massey. It was a great book but I thought I'd give it a rest and try and listen to the radio. I guessed that the person that rented the car previously listened to gospel because as soon as I pressed the FM band button, Kirk Franklin's "Imagine Me" flooded the car. Although I had heard the song before, I never really listened to the words. I found myself absorbing the lyrics and the sentiment as if I were a sponge. I began to sing along as it ministered to me. Although, I kept lifting my right hand to turn it off or to change the channel, I couldn't complete the action. It was as if someone or something was keeping me from doing so. When I heard the part "What your father did," I stiffened. "All gone…all gone…."

What a song, I thought to myself. Looking ahead at the sky, I wondered why that song came on.

Behold, I will bring health and cure them and reveal unto them the abundance of peace and truth.

There it was again.

If I had been honest with myself, I would have known and recognized that the Lord was trying to get through to me but it didn't make it to my frontal lobe and as a result, I shrugged off the message that the voice was trying to convey. Dad was wrong and would continue to be wrong. He had better have one heck of story for me to really forgive him. Justin had often said that I could hold onto a grudge light-years longer than I could hold onto a dollar. I felt myself nodding in agreement to what Justin said. I am sure that that was not something that I should have been proud of but at that moment, I didn't care.

I don't know why, but I began to think of the Thanksgiving dinner that turned the tide for me.

It was a cold Thanksgiving Day and no one seemed thankful for anything. Mom had to work that afternoon so she cooked the day before to make sure that we had a great meal with all of the fixings. I remembered that when I awoke that morning to get to the football field for the game, that it was a dreary day. That should have been my first clue.

I was a senior in high school and my sisters and I went to the homecoming game. I was in the marching band so I had to be there. When the game was over, I ran into the gymnasium and grabbed my jacket out of the locker. Once putting on my jacket, I secured my flute case and rushed to meet my sisters after the game. Karlie was standing with them because we all walked home from the games together.

"Hey, guys," I said. I was happy that the game was over. It was cold standing in the bleachers. The wind was blowing unusually hard and it seemed to be always blowing in my direction. Although I wasn't looking forward to going home, I was hungry and enjoyed laughing and joking with my sisters and Karlie during our walk home.

"The band looked and sounded good today. It's no wonder you guys won the state championships. I know you were really worried about Sun Valley High," Celia said. She was a musician as well but she played the cello. She would drive to some of the band competitions to support me when she was home for the weekend from college.

"Yeah, I think that we did good," I agreed and smiled at Celia, secretly thanking her for the compliment. "I would have loved for Mom to be here to walk out on the field with me today during halftime. This was the last time I would be playing in the band," I said regretfully. "I really wanted her to be here with me and all of the other graduating seniors."

"Well, you know she had to work and Daddy had already committed to bringing food to less fortunate for the holiday," Loni said. "I hope that he isn't home when we get home. You know he will bring someone home with him from the church just to show that he is charitable." Loni rolled her eyes in disgust.

"I know. Let's just make the best of it, okay," I said, hoping that we could change the subject and converse about lighter and less somber topics.

"Dag, you guys need to be happy that you have your father with you. I mean, he is living in the same house. At least he visible," Karlie stated. Anger and a littler resentment traced her words.

"Karlie, the man you see and the man that we see are two different people," Darlene added.

"Alright. Let's not have a rag-on-Dad afternoon," I said.

"Ooooh, look at Moses Longfield," Karlie cooed as she followed Moses' delicious midnight physique to the waiting car. Moses was a junior at my high school. I had a minor "thing" for him but because he was a junior, I didn't pursue it. How would it look for me, a senior, mooning over a junior?

"Yeah, he is quite the specimen," I acknowledged. I unknowingly licked my lips. He turned around and our eyes met. He caught me mid-lick and smiled. Embarrassed, I just waved; he waved back and jumped into the car.

Walking through the major shopping district of our city, we did a little window-shopping. Karlie told us that she was going to her father's house for dinner and her mother was not happy about it. Her mother had been complaining about her father all day. Her father was chairman of the deacon board at his church but he hadn't stopped his whoremongering ways. I looked at Karlie and shook my head.

"These fake Christians are a trip," I said aloud as I thought about the many deacons that had their little sideline women.

We waved to Karlie when she turned down her street. "I'll talk to you tomorrow so that we can catch the bus to go to the mall," I told her.

Karlie looked at me with a crazed expression.

Comprehending her message, I responded, "I know we don't have any money to spend on Black Friday, but it will get us out of the house," I explained.

"I hear ya, girl. I'm in," Karlie said. "Talk to you tomorrow."

Upon entering the house, Darlene immediately shed her coat and headed for the kitchen. She promised Mom that she would make sure that dinner was ready by 5:00 p.m. It was 3:00 p.m.

Not longer after Darlene, Loni and Celia prepared everything for dinner, Dad walked in. He was without a guest and we were shocked. Usually Dad was a little easier to be around when he was performing for someone from the congregation.

"Is dinner ready?" he asked, without a greeting.

"It should be ready in twenty minutes," Darlene responded flatly.

"That's good. Did you win?" he asked and turned to look at me. I was in the dining room placing the silverware on the table unaware that he was speaking to me until I felt his eyes on my back.

"Yes, we won and I received a plaque for Outstanding Section Leader," I proclaimed proudly. "I really wish that you or Mom could have been there for the halftime graduating senior presentations."

His eyes darkened and the face that almost yielded a smile hardened. I didn't think that it could look any stonier. "You know that I have obligations at the church. I am not going to apologize for being needed there," he spat.

I decided to continue setting the table. When I was done, I walked through the living area into the kitchen.

Nothing else was said for about fifteen minutes. Darlene broke the silence when she announced that dinner was ready.

Celia and I sat down at the table. It looked beautiful. Loni and Darlene bought beautiful autumn decorations to add a color to the table. Although all of the food looked scrumptious and the room looked festive, none of us had the demeanor of cheer. Darlene brought in the turkey and handed Dad the electric knife as she plugged it into the outlet. Dad carved the turkey and sat down. Darlene brought in the crescent rolls and the cranberry sauce. Finally, all of the necessary items were on the table.

I looked across the table at Celia. Her head was bowed as if praying. Because I was sitting directly across from her, I kicked her under the table. Her head popped up like a jack-in-the-box. I gave her a "What's up with you?" look. She shook her head to communicate that nothing was the matter but I knew better. Her eyes shone signs of fear as if she knew a storm was brewing.

"Let's us ask the blessing over the food that your mother cooked. Oh, and thank you, Darlene, for finishing the meal. I am sure that your mother would be proud. Girls, the table looks really nice." Dad smiled at us. I couldn't believe that he was smiling. Was he in his "public" character? I found myself looking around to be certain that no one else was in the room. No. No one was there, just the family, save Mom.

"Thank you, Dad," we all said. Because we said it almost simultaneously, we sounded like a first-grade class greeting their teacher. We looked at each other confused by Dad's behavior and compliments.

"Gracious Father, we thank you for the food that we are about to consume. We thank you for making provisions for this family and allowing us to see another Thanksgiving Day together. We thank you for the chef and the chef's assistants. Continue to bless this family. Lord, we may not be all that we want to be or should be…"

During Dad's prayer, I was really trying to communicate with the Lord because there were problems at church and the new pastor and my relationship with Jesus was at a crossroad. I was allowing myself to be happy about the compliments that were just made and began to think positively. Knowing that I was not what I wanted to be in Christ, I silently resolved to try and do better.

When Dad said, "We may not be what we want to be or should be,"

97

I agreed and said "Amen" aloud, acknowledging my own shortcomings. After I said that, I heard Darlene gasp and then a chair move. The sound of feet moving in my direction began to get louder. I opened my eyes and saw my dad coming toward me. The scowl on his face resembled an angry bull that was about to pummel the unsuspecting matador. Before I had an opportunity to stand and run, his fist connected with my mouth and I flew off of the chair onto the floor. My elbows broke my fall and my behind hit the floor.

"Stop!" Darlene screamed as Dad hovered over me.

"Who are you to judge me?" he shouted. "I am doing the best I can."

"What are you talking about?" I whispered through tears. I lifted my hand to my stinging lip. It was throbbing and there was pain with each pulsation. I was shocked to realize that I could feel the residual heat from the blow. I was even more confused by his outburst.

"I was talking about myself and my walk with God. He knows that I can do better and I was agreeing with you," I heard myself yell as I began to stand, feeling a little lightheaded. "Are you feeling that guilty about yourself and your life that you have to knock around your own daughter because you know that you have fallen so short? What is wrong with you?" My feelings of detestation increased with each second that I stood looking at my dad.

Who is this man? I thought. Why did God allow this man to continue in his supposed service? How could Dad even look at himself in the mirror? I was having a conversation with God and as a result I got attacked by one of His people? What kind of God was I serving?

A car horn was blaring when I shook off the memory. The lady's face in the sleek black Acura behind me was distorted as she leaned on her horn. The light had turned green. I quickly added pressure to the accelerator and moved forward. Making a left into the hospital parking lot, I remembered that I had to face Dad in a few moments. I wasn't sure if I wanted to look at him and decided that I'd better touch base with Justin. Hearing his voice always calmed me. I knew that I needed strength to talk with the man who gave me life.

"Hey, what are you doing?" I said to Justin in greeting when he picked up on the second ring.

"Hi, babe. Where are you? I thought that you were coming straight in?" Justin asked.

"That was my plan but traffic was so backed up that I though it would be easier to just stop by the hospital to see how Mom was today before I headed home," I explained. There was a long silence.

"Justin, are you there?" I was beginning to get the feeling that something was wrong.

"I am here. I just wanted to be there with you when you went to see your mom."

"Thanks, sweetie, but I am here now. Have you picked up Adam from camp?" It was close to 5:00 p.m. and I knew that Adam was used to me picking him around this time. He was probably watching the door to see if I was going to walk through.

"As a matter of fact, I am on my way there. I just left the office."

"Okay, well, I'll visit with Mom for an hour or so and then I'll come home. Can you guys wait for me to eat or did you want to get something?"

"Why don't we meet you at the hospital and go out and get something afterwards," Justin suggested.

"That'll work." His voice seemed a little weird.

"Is everything okay?" I inquired. "Is there something that I should know before I go into the hospital?" My mind was beginning to visualize an empty bed and Nurse Anne looking at me with a grave expression. "Justin…"

"It's just that your mom has not regained consciousness and now the doctors are stating that she has lapsed into a coma." Each word that Justin stated was tentative but clearly enunciated.

"Why a coma?" I asked.

"I guess her vitals have not been good and she is not responding to anything anymore," Justin said almost apologetically.

"Oh, my goodness. I had no idea that it was going to get this bad. Has anyone called Darlene, Celia or Loni?"

"Your father has called them and I am surprised you didn't see their cars in the parking lot. They have been there since noon today."

"Nobody thought to call me?" I almost screamed.

"No. We purposely didn't call you because you had already planned to be there this evening and I wanted to be with you when Dr. Jamison gave you the news." Justin exhaled audibly. "Should I come now and ask Ms. Debbie to watch Adam for a little while? She said that she would be available."

"I guess so. Please do what you think is best. I have got to get in there to see what is going on. If Ms. Debbie is available, Adam will be fine with staying with her for a while." My mind was racing and I quickly wanted to end the call. "Call me when you are on your way, okay. Thanks for trying to warn me."

"Be strong, Paige. I'll be there shortly," Justin said.

I could feel my eyes stinging, warning me that tears had been summoned to make an appearance. I couldn't go in the hospital with red eyes. "You better not cry," I told myself in a shaky voice. My purse was on the floor on the passenger side. I grabbed my black leather purse and placed it on my lap. I opened it to retrieve a tissue. Dabbing my eyes to dam the water, I admonished myself for letting the liquid escape. After the lipstick and a little face powder were applied, I exited the car and walked quickly toward the hospital's entrance.

Chapter 15

I walked slowly through the automatic sliding doors, not sure if I wanted to actually go to Mom's room. Once reaching the nurses' station, I greeted Nurse Ann with a tight smile. I knew that it wasn't convincing but I felt the need to acknowledge her. If I attempted to part my lips to say anything, I would break down.

Mom, comatose? It was unbelievable.

Wordlessly, Nurse Ann reached out for me and touched my hand. I covered her hand with my own. After a couple of moments, I removed my shaking hand and made my way to the room. Loni was standing against the wall at the far end of the room as if afraid to get closer to Mom. *A comatose state is not contagious,* I thought. *Why is she standing over there like that?* Walking closer to her, I noticed that her eyes were red and swollen, apparently from crying.

"Loni," I said, unsure if she was mentally in the room.

She turned her head slowly and looked at me while returning to reality. "Is she going to die, Paige?" She sounded like a child inquiring about an injured puppy but she resembled a raccoon courtesy of her mascara. All I could do was embrace her.

"I don't know, sweetheart. We have to believe that she wants to come back to us," I said. It was the only answer that I could produce. "I know that we need to think positive, okay? Let's not lose it."

She looked at me, nodded and held my hands tightly. Her hands were clammy and cold.

"I will try, Paige. I need her so much. I am pregnant," she said with a tear streaming down her soiled cheek. Her eyes were smiling but the rest of her face was stoic.

"That is wonderful!" I exclaimed in a muffled scream. I hugged her again and felt a tear on my cheek as well.

Loni never thought that she would have any children. This was great news. *Mom has got to come out of this. She has just has to,* I thought.

"I guess that job in Texas is out of the question," I said, almost relieved.

"At least for now," she said.

I think that she was a bit relieved as well. The thought of having a baby so far away from family wouldn't be an ideal situation for Loni.

"What are the two of you smiling about?" Tyler asked as he entered the room with Dad, holding two cups of what I assumed was coffee.

I motioned to him while rubbing my tummy to let him know that I knew the secret. The gesture registered and he smiled proudly.

"Forget it. You Hunter girls are always keeping secrets," Tyler said.

Loni walked over to him to get the coffee and nudged him playfully. I think talking about the baby temporarily brightened her spirits.

I walked over to Mom's bedside and look at her. "Mom, please don't leave us. You are so loved and needed here. Fight to come back to us. I love you," I whispered close to her ear.

I started to think of how happy she would be when she found out about Loni. She would certainly give her Jesus the credit. She had been praying that Loni would be able to conceive and always said that God would answer prayer. I wouldn't refute Mom's faith because I once had that same belief. Why wouldn't God allow Mom to be a part of this happy time? It is so hard to believe in a God who seems to always throw so many curves. *Are we being prepared somehow to live without Mom in our lives? Is she going to die?* I asked myself.

This sickness is not unto death but for the Glory of God that the Son might be glorified thereby.

Hearing that, I abruptly stood and turned to Loni, Dad and Tyler and said, "Mom is not going to die." Not knowing at the time where I heard the statement, I was confident that what was just communicated was undeniably true. Crazily enough, I didn't know why I was so sure, but I was. Not wanting to ask Dad for biblical confirmation, I kissed Mom quickly and made my way to the corridor to call Karlie.

I looked at Loni and told her that I'd be right back.

"Where are you going?" she asked.

"I've got to make a phone call," I responded as I quickly made my way to an area that was close to a window.

"Karlie, when I was standing over Mom's bed wondering whether or not we need to prepare ourselves for the worst, I heard it," I spoke rapidly, almost excitedly.

"Really?" she said. Her voice was an octave higher than usual. She was more keyed up than me.

"I had to call you because I recognized the phrase but I wasn't sure if it was my hope talking or something."

"Well, what did the voice say?" she inquired

"'This sickness is not unto death but for the Glory of God that the Son might be glorified thereby,'" I repeated. "Isn't that somewhere in the gospels?"

"Yeah, I have to check and I'll call you back," she said, sounding energized.

"I can wait. I'll hold," I almost begged.

"No, girl. I'll have to call you back. I haven't heard you this excited about researching the bible in a while. This is almost like old times, Paige," she said, laughing at my lack of patience re-emerging. I used to have a real hunger for the bible. Trying to decipher what different passages meant and how they could be applied to my life was also an adventure. That was a lifetime ago it seemed. For now, I only wanted to confirm the origin of the words that I'd just heard.

"Okay, call me back as soon as you can," I said

"I will. This is great, Paige. Try to think of the other things that you have been hearing and we I can look them up too," she quickly added. "Gotta go. Bye."

I walked slowly back to Mom's room. Dad was standing in the

doorway. He was obviously waiting for me. I had forgotten all about our "talk." I stopped about three feet from him and looked at him waiting for him to make the first move.

"You know we have to talk," he reminded me.

"Yes, I am aware of that. I just got so caught up with Loni and seeing Mom in that condition. It is really tough on all of us. I guess it has to be hardest of all on you after all you…" I stopped myself from daddy-bashing and decided to let him speak.

"Well, I guess I need to take a portion of the blame but that isn't what I want to talk to you about," he said, shifting from one foot to another. He would not meet my gaze.

"Where do you want to have this conversation?" I asked.

He looked around and pointed toward the lounge that I'd just left.

"Is it okay if we talk in there?"

I agreed with a nod.

"Let me just tell Loni where we are. Celia and Darlene are in the cafeteria," he informed, before he turned to walked back into the room. He whispered into Loni's ear. She looked at me and nodded. She was sitting in a beige chair with wooden arms. Tyler stood against the lime green walls with his hands on Loni's shoulders, moving them in a circular soothing motion. Our eyes met and he smiled as if he already knew what I was going to hear but I knew he hadn't.

Dad extended his hand in the direction of the lounge as if to say, "After you." I walked in front of him toward the room. I began to feel a little nervous about what Dad was going to disclose.

He found a chair and sat down. I sat down on the other side of the round maple table. I looked at the table, noticing the scratches and the imperfections. *Talk about a visual foreshadowing of his story. Scratches and imperfections. Oh well,* I thought to myself, *let's get on with it.*

"Paige!"

I heard what sounded like Justin's voice coming from outside the lounge. I stood and peeked outside the lounge entrance and saw Justin approaching me.

"Hey, babe. I was just about to have a conversation with Dad," I said to Justin as he closed the gap between us. I looked at him with gratitude.

He recognized the expression displayed on my face. I hugged him tightly lingering in his embrace for longer than usual. I could feel his muscular outline under his gray shirt. His cologne of choice for the day, "Cool Water," lingered lightly but I could still smell the soap. I hadn't realized how much I needed him until now.

He stepped back from me and looked into my eyes as if confirming what he saw only a few moments ago. He whispered, "You are not ready for this. Let's go sit with your mom for now." I nodded as he took my hand and led me back toward Mom's room.

Darlene and Celia returned and were standing by Mom's bed. Dad entered the room not long after we sat down. Justin led him out of the room and probably explained that he didn't think that I should be encumbered with any other matters. His conversation with me would have to wait. Not many minutes passed when they both returned. Dad's expression was tight and his jaw muscle was visible through his unusually taut skin. He wasn't happy but he said nothing.

I explained to Celia and Darlene that I was confident that Mom was not going to die. I don't think that they believed me.

They would simply have to wait and see, I told myself.

"Loni said that you acted as if you just knew. That doesn't sound like you, Paige. How can you be so sure?" Darlene asked. Her face was contorted into a look that screamed confusion and desperation.

"If I told you how I knew, you wouldn't believe me. I can hardly believe that I am putting any stock into it as well but I am holding onto any glimmer of hope," I said, not wanting to tell them that I heard it my heart.

I wasn't sure how I heard it but it was just like the other voice that I had been hearing lately. They had begun to get more distinguishable each time. My rational mind refused to believe that it was the inner witness or the Holy Spirit speaking to me. I had not given any credence to God, Jesus or the Holy Spirit for years. Why now? Again, my confusion was getting the better of me and frustration made a house call to my psyche which caused me to want to change the subject so that I didn't have to think about the voice or what it meant.

"I don't care how you know, Paige, I just hope that you are right. I didn't think that you prayed anymore and you seemed to not want to have anything to do with Jesus," Celia reasoned. "You had better not be dealing with the occult or anything like that."

I looked at her like she had certainly lost her mind. "Now you know that I would not get involved any crazy mess like that. Mom would be disappointed and although I don't talk to God anymore…" I sighed, shook my head and decided not to continue. "Let's not get too crazy."

I was wondering what was taking Karlie so long to get back to me and so I decided that I would kill time by checking my work v-mail. I had been gone all day and knew that someone wanted or needed something from me.

I informed Justin that I was going to use the phone and left the room.

Dad grabbed my arm when I made a left down the corridor.

"I can understand that you may not be up to our talk but we must do it soon."

I looked at the hand grasping my naked flesh and then turned my attention skyward because I was about to lose all decorum. All of my childhood memories made themselves visible in my mind's eye.

"Dad, let go of my arm," I demanded in a low but clearly venomous voice.

He immediately released my arm as if it was suddenly on fire and stepped back. He looked at me with fear and a hint of contrition.

"I am sorry. I just wanted to get your attention."

He quickly looked into the room to be sure that no one was alarmed by our exchange.

Tiring of hearing about his need to cleanse and purge his guilt, I rolled my eyes, looked him squarely in the eye and told him, "We will talk when the time is right. Today is not the right time. I am not entirely sure when the right time will be, but please don't continue to harass me about this. Mom is my main concern. She should be yours."

Without allowing him the opportunity to say anything further, I turned on my heels and walked down the hall in hopes of getting a good signal to use my cell phone. As I walked away, I felt relieved that I wouldn't have to participate in the dreaded conversation with Dad. I was so glad that Justin was able see that I was not up to talking with Dad.

Thankfully, he was able to gauge my mental state even when I couldn't. I dialed my office phone to retrieve any voice mails that were left during the day. I pressed the number one to play them. "Paige, this is June; when you get this message and it is not after 6:00 p.m., please call me. I simply want to touch base with you about the Rosenfeld account and the meeting this morning." June's voice sounded a little excited. I twisted my wrist to check my watch and it was about 5:40 p.m. My first instinct was to wait until tomorrow to call June but because I felt that I had good news to share, I didn't see the need to wait. I hadn't any other urgent messages so I completed the review of the messages and dialed June's number.

"Hi, June, Paige Covington here. I received your voice mail message and wanted to catch you before you left the office for the day."

"Paige, I'm glad that you were able to call me back. I am taking a vacation day tomorrow and wanted to discuss the Rosenfeld meeting this morning." Her voice seemed tentative and she sounded as if she was choosing her words carefully.

"I would have thought Myra would have given you the good news," I said. "The client communicated that they liked the presentation for the most part. We have some minor changes to make but as a whole it was what they were looking for. I think that we may have to sell them on the idea that other people who have the same role as I would be presenting the material at the various different Rosenfeld locations, but I think we can make that a win as well."

I realized that I was rambling on about the meeting and thought that I'd better stop talking and find out if she had any questions. "Is there anything that you wanted to know?"

June exhaled. "Paige, I had a conversation with Myra and she said that the client, although they thought your detailed explanation of the product was very well done, felt that you seemed a little abrasive when answering their inquiries about the product."

She paused apparently to let that sink in. "Myra mentioned that you led the meeting but did not allow the team to have an active role. The client wanted to hear from the other attendees but said that you provided answers to their questions as if the group was not there."

I began to feel heat rising to my face and leaned against the window, stunned.

"June, I have to say that I am astonished by this report. I was under the impression that the meeting went very well and that Myra wanted me to lead the meeting. She even commented after the client visit that she was pleased. What sense would it make for me to create and execute the presentation and have another person answer the questions posed that related to the information I had just outlined? Myra informed me clearly during our prep call that this was my meeting and that any questions relating to the product should be in my court. Anything outside of the actual product or network, meaning the rates information, would be handled by either her or Leann." I took a breath to allow her to respond to my rebuttal, fully cognizant of the fact that my voice revealed a little more than annoyance.

"Paige, believe me, I understand that you may feel that I am blindsiding you with this but I simply wanted to hear your side. I have also talked with Leann and she basically said the same thing that you have just said. At this point, going forward, I want you to tread lightly when it comes to this account. Myra has a good relationship with them and she doesn't want anything to compromise this opportunity or her position with her contacts and any additional business that can be gleaned for her and our organization."

Oh, so that was it, I realized silently.

I couldn't believe what I was hearing. Was I being asked to shut my mouth and act like a trained monkey with this client so that Myra could make her commission? I knew that the vibe that I received from the Rosenfeld team was negative. The reason for this issue couldn't be because I am African-American, could it? That would be the only viable explanation.

Screw this, I thought. "What exactly do you want me to do, June? I am not understanding what you mean by 'treading lightly.'" I wanted her to simply state what she wanted me to do.

"For now, let Myra lead the conversations with the client. They aren't comfortable with you because you are new to the account. It is obvious to all that you are capable but we don't want to cause any ripples and take the client out of their comfort zone right now," she said.

I don't think that she even believed or knew what she was saying. I sure didn't.

Always riding the fence. It was apparent that she was worried about any backlash that might result if Myra didn't make her money. Silence the little black girl. I couldn't believe that I was once again dealing with hypocrites. At least they didn't claim to be Christians.

Unfortunately that didn't stop the feeling of betrayal and the wave of nausea from churning in my belly.

"Will the client contact Myra and Leann only going forward?" I asked, almost wanting that to be the procedure.

"No. The client will be contacting you for the enrollment and communications schedule that you discussed and also the coordination of the open enrollment meetings but Myra will sometimes be the person delivering the answers simply to be sure that the answers provided are what the client wants to hear."

What? I thought. I guess it didn't matter if the answers provided were wrong.

This was nonsense. It was my turn to audibly exhale.

"June, this makes absolutely no sense. I must say that this will not serve as a panacea and will certainly pose a problem in the future."

There was no way that I was going to stay on this account and be relegated to act as a glorified go-between. If the client was not comfortable with me, because I was Black, no doubt, then June needed to get another representative to replace me on Rosenfeld.

"I understand your point of view, Paige, but let's just do things this way until things settle down." She said these words as if someone was standing over her with a gun, forcing her to say each word verbatim.

Liar, is what I wanted to scream but instead I asked derisively, "I guess I haven't any choice at this juncture, do I?" I inhaled and began to tune her out completely. "June, I have to go. I am at the hospital. Enjoy your day off. I am sure that we'll be talking next week."

"Have a good weekend, Paige, and I hope that your mother is better soon."

Anxious to get of the phone with her so that I could scream, I calmly said, "Thanks, June. Goodbye."

I silently talked myself out of calling Myra and giving her an earful. "This company is becoming a trip," I said aloud as I flipped my cell phone shut.

That Myra was a pill. I didn't know if I was going to be able to deal with her much longer.

Chapter 16

I guess my face displayed a mixture of profound anger and confusion when I turned corner and made my way into Mom's room, because upon my entrance, all eyes were on me.

"What is the matter? Something wrong at work?" Justin asked. He mirrored my confusion as he walked toward me.

"I am just being reminded that I am a minority. It has been made clear that I am just window dressing."

Shaking my head to dismiss the need to converse about the matter, I said "I'll talk to you about it later."

My attention turned to my dad and sisters. "I am going to get going. We have to pick up Adam from Ms. Debbie and it has been a long day."

I hugged each of them except Dad and walked toward the door. I didn't feel that I should show him any affection or compassion. I can't remember every feeling any warmth from him. My heart seemed heavier not only because of Mom but because of my relationship with Dad.

Like a faint breeze, familiar words seem to be written with a soft quill onto my heart.

When my father and my mother forsake me, then the Lord will take me up.

I stopped and let the words become real to me. Where is this coming from? Mom had never forsaken me but Dad sure had. I knew that was from the bible. I looked back at Dad, realizing that I was being disobedient but not caring and left the room.

I rolled over and looked up at the ceiling and was visited once again by the feeling that had become a constant reminder that I was alone. I knew that I had my husband and child but I still felt that I was always battling. This added to the emptiness. It left me mentally and physically tired. What was I fighting and why hadn't I figured out how to quell all of my crazy emotions?

The situation with work wasn't helping. Was I working for a company that permitted such blatant hypocrisy? I guess I did. Did I attract liars and phonies? I closed my eyes and decided that I would get out of bed. Sitting on the side of the bed I stopped and looked over at my book shelf. The moon shone through the large window and seemed to spotlight a particular book on the shelf. I squinted to see what book was being illuminated courtesy of the night's sky. Standing to my feet, I slowly walked toward the shelves and was almost shocked to find that the book that shone as clear as day was the bible, my old bible. I thought that I had given it away when I moved back home from college. My hand reached for it but quickly retreated as if being told that it would burn me if I touched it. I once again reached toward it and placed my fingers tentatively on its spine. My mother had given it to me at my college graduation. Tears sprang to my eyes when I thought about how proud Mom was when she gave it to me. She knew that I had stopped going to church regularly while in school but she never gave up hope that I'd return to God. She never gave up me.

I dropped to the floor but left the bible in its place. *I can't go there. I don't want to be misled or mislead anyone. I just wanted to feel whole and to know the peace that I had when I was younger,* I thought.

"What are you doing on the floor?" Justin whispered, standing over me.

"I can't sleep. Dad has been hounding me to share his autobiography…Mom hasn't regained consciousness and it has been over two weeks since Dr. Jamison stated that she was essentially comatose." I shifted my weight to extend my leg and sat squarely on my behind. "Work has become even more crazy than unusual and I am coming apart at the seams. I really need some help." The words tumbled out of my mouth without a breath in between. I leaned into to Justin's chest once he joined me on the carpet.

"Paige, I have been thinking that maybe you need to take a couple of days off."

I jerked, poised to disagree.

"I know that you don't want to but I think that you need a rest." His eyes were gentle but his voice was assertive and I knew that he wouldn't take no for an answer.

"Okay," I said. I was tired and didn't want to argue. I'd call June in the morning and schedule to take the next two days off.

"Good. Thanks for not giving me a hard time," he said rising to his feet. "By the way, I ran into an old friend. You wouldn't believe that Daniel Manders is now living in the area. And," Justin paused for effect then said, "he is a pastor of a church. Can you believe that ?!" He was smiling from ear to ear. Daniel was Justin's buddy. For some reason they lost touch and now he was back in our lives. I wondered why he didn't contact us to tell us that he was moving back to the area.

"I know you are happy that your roadie is back in town. I can't wait to see him. Is he married?"

Justin turned to me while getting into the bed and smirked.

"Yes, and he seems very happy about it."

"I am glad for him," I said.

"Come back to bed," Justin chided.

I used the foot of the bed to stand to my feet and get into the bed. Once under the comforter, I allowed Justin to wrap me in his arms. I was still thinking about the void that seemed to plague me but I closed my eyes and tried to wish it away.

The next day, after being treated to a big breakfast, Justin and I stopped by Home Depot to pick out some paint after making an impromptu decision that we would paint the kitchen. We decided on a pale, almost sage green. At the check-out counter, Justin reached for my hand.

"I've talked to Daniel again and he has invited us to his church. He is the pastor at Zion House." I think that he sensed my apprehension and added, "The church is non-denominational and Daniel made a point in telling me that it is not chock full of the mores that you would find in the traditional African-American church."

He pulled me close and I looked around to see if anyone was staring at Justin's outward show of affection. His index finger was gently placed under my chin. He brought my face to his and his eyes looked into mine with what I think I recognized as need. If he really wanted to go to this church, why not? I thought. It sounded like it wasn't anything like the churches of my youth. Justin never really mentioned going to church although I knew that he went with his family as a child. Because I was so opposed to it, we never went. I guess I was the reason that Adam had not been exposed to church except when he went with Mom.

As Adam chatted with the cashier, my phone rang and it was Karlie. I motioned to Justin that I would be standing outside because of the phone call and he nodded.

"Hey there, girl," I said.

"Hi, Paige. I just wanted to follow up with you. I know that we confirmed that some of the phrases that you have been hearing have been scriptures but I am a little concerned about you not wanting to do anything about what seems to be the Holy Spirit speaking to you," she said.

"Well, just because we proved that the words have their origin in the bible, doesn't mean that I exactly have to do anything."

I didn't like where this conversation was going.

"Paige, reconnect yourself with the Master," she stated, somewhat seriously.

"What, Karlie?" I asked, almost hurt. I didn't understand why she was pushing me to make a decision that caused some much angst.

She exhaled impatiently. "I have to go but you have heard from Him not once but twice; probably more times that you are admitting to me, and you mean to tell me that you are not running to the altar? Can't you understand that He is the key to unlock the feelings of emptiness?"

"Not exactly." I heard Karlie suck her teeth. "Anyway, I do have some news that may make you happy. Justin's friend, Daniel, has moved back to town and has a church, Zion House. The family is going to church this Sunday."

"Well, that is something, "Karlie said with a chuckle.

"Yeah, I don't want Justin to go without me."

"Zion House is the church that I was telling you about. You should have a good time." The intonation of her voice was noticeably different. She now seemed at ease.

"I hope that Justin does," I said, not wanting to get my hopes up.

"I know Adam will. He seems to love being in church."

"Sounds good. I've gotta go. Call me Sunday evening to let me know how service was."

I saw Justin out of the corner of my eye walking toward me with the cart of paint. He was smiling at me, making me feel a little uncomfortable.

Why couldn't I just let him love me or even admire me? I was always watching the way other people looked at me and what others thought. I was so unnecessarily self-conscious. This too had to stop. I was determined to open myself to receive the love that he wanted so desperately to give me. I really needed to get past the trust issue.

Once arriving at the house, Justin changed his clothes.

I sat on the bed and watched him as he put on his white dress shirt and tied his tie. He always looked good when going to the office. I secretly wished he would stay home with me for the rest of the day but he was nice enough to take the morning off so that we could talk over breakfast about Mom and what the next steps were.

He believed strongly and tried to convince me that it was the Lord speaking to me. He even opened up the bible to show me the scripture in the Gospel of John that I heard convincing me that Mom was going to pull through. It was right there in black in white; the same exact words that I'd heard. He didn't understand, however, why she had yet not regained consciousness. And as a result, my resolve was getting a bit shaky.

I finally told him pieces of how I'd been feeling but not everything. I'd mentioned that I had been flooded with memories and didn't know why. He was patient while I talked and didn't make any judgments.

Regardless of what I told him, his expression remained the same. Thinking about how he held my gaze with love and concern as I replayed some of the memories made me love him even more. I felt so much closer to Justin after being able to release all of the pent-up issues that caused me to distance myself from him. As he stood to leave the bedroom, he placed a small peck on my lips. When our mouths parted, I smiled and kissed him again and allowed my lips to part. He followed my example. The kiss deepened and I rose to place my arms around his neck.

We continued our sensuous tongue dance until he stopped the kiss and said, "What are you doing, Mrs. Covington?" He was smiling at me. "I have a three o'clock meeting that I can't miss."

"I am just showing you how much I love you, you sweet, sexy business man," I said in a low sultry voice.

"Well, well," he returned, almost laughing as his hand lowered to my backside. "I'd like to see some more but I have to get to work."

Because he was the manager of the e-technology department at a thriving communications company, as well as being one of the managing partners, he was always in meetings and making deals. I slowly removed his hands from my behind and began to remove my blouse, button by button. I didn't lose eye contact with him as my shirt (one of his old ones that I stole) fell to the carpet. He continued to watch me as I stepped out of my jeans. I stood before him in my turquoise bra and underwear, which thankfully matched and allowed him to drink in the sight of me for just a moment. Knowing that I had a pouch, feelings of inferiority tried to creep into my mind. I closed that mental door and locked it.

Holding in my tummy and looking at Justin from under my eyelashes, I said, "When you are right, you are right, husband. You do have some work to do." I walked over to him and immediately his hands found their way around my waist and we kissed hungrily. I treated myself to the task of removing his belt and unbuttoning his pants. His shirt was easily removed from his body and we fell onto the bed. The impact onto the bed was harder than expected and we laughed out loud. *This felt so right,* I thought.

The kisses and nibbles on my neck and shoulders were welcome. He captured my mouth again and my breath was taken.

His mouth is most sweet. Yes, he is altogether lovely. He is my beloved and this is my friend.

He looked into my eyes with so much raw emotion that I felt my chest heaving. I was near tears because my heart was full of love for him. As he lay atop of me, I felt the star of the show making an appearance. The curtain went up for a performance that would prove to be worthy of an award.

After two curtain calls, I finally let Justin leave for work. He'd be on time for his meeting but I hoped that he remained awake. I smiled to myself and rolled over, inviting sleep to consume me.

My beloved is mine and I am his…

After arriving home from the hospital I was feeling a little disappointed that Mom was still unresponsive. I decided to make a nice dinner for the family. Keeping my mind on something other that life's disappointments would help. Dad had not mentioned the need for us to talk but it looked as if Mom's condition was taking a toll on him. He looked haggard. My offer to bring him dinner at the hospital continued to be declined. I am sure that he had a number of people cooking for him but I thought that as his daughter, I should present the option. I was beginning to get worried about him. I was also beginning to doubt the words that were seemingly whispered into me. I know that I heard the voice correctly but the longer Mom was there, without movement, my resolve was losing its power. Doubt and uncertainty entered my mind.

They that wait upon the Lord will renew their strength. Wait, I say, Wait on the Lord.

A smile crept onto my face. I was finally coming to the realization that God's words that had been deeply buried in me were making their way to the surface. It was doing this without my permission.

While changing into something a little more comfortable, I walked into my office and saw that I had three messages.

"Nope," I said to myself aloud and turned to leave the office. "I promised that I wouldn't work and I am not," I said once again aloud, showing telltale signs of lunacy.

I replayed the conversation that I had with June last week. Thankfully, I didn't sense too much opposition when I informed her that I'd be taking a couple of days off. I think that she realized that I wouldn't be coerced into putting this off. Since my meeting with Rosenfeld, I hadn't had very much interaction with Myra but Leann knew something was up. She either decided to wait for me to tell her or had arrived at the conclusion that it wasn't any of her business. I still couldn't get over it. I was still surprised that in this day and age there were people that were made uncomfortable with an assertive black woman. I was not looking forward to work on Monday. I made a pact with myself that I wouldn't think about it anymore and focus on getting dinner on the table.

My men were happily surprised by the meal that awaited them when they walked in the door. Justin called me to let me know that he would be picking up Adam from camp since I dropped him off. He also made sure that he thanked me for our midday tryst.

With his signature smile, Adam greeted me with a hug and a big zerbert. I introduced him to that after watching it on the Cosby show. The character Rudy made it famous when she would kiss her father, portrayed by Bill Cosby. My child is the joy of my life. He isn't an angel by any means but he certainly had my heart.

"Why are you smiling, Mom?" he asked as he kicked off his sandals. He was clothed in an orange cotton tank top and a pair of jean shorts. He continued to smile as I greeted Justin with a lingering kiss.

"Don't start anything you can't finish, wife," Justin murmured into my ear, careful not to let Adam hear.

I laughed and pushed him away. "Wash your hands, dinner is ready."

Justin tapped my backside, "Junk in the truck!"

"Nasty," I teased.

Adam loved pasta; he didn't care what kind. My chicken and broccoli in a cheese sauce over colored fettuccini received rave reviews. He hadn't mastered spinning the pasta into his fork but the food eventually made it into his mouth as well as on his shirt. Once Justin announced that we were going to church on Sunday as a family, Adam became excited about going. He made it clear that he wanted to wear a tie. Justin made plans with Daniel to go out for dinner after service. After loading the dishwasher, I made a mental note that I had to pick up a pair of dress shoes for Adam and Justin tomorrow. I'd throw in a new dress shirt for Adam and maybe a simple dress for me.

Justin seemed really excited about attending church. He kept saying that he really missed church and hearing the Word on a regular basis. I tried to hide my apprehension. I was actually afraid to go to the Zion House. I was afraid of what I would see and most importantly, how I would react.

I couldn't renege now.

Chapter 17

"Why the furrowed brow? After this afternoon, you should be smiling for days," Justin said as he came up behind me.

"Just not looking forward to going back to the hospital tomorrow," I replied softly. "Dad looked bad today. I just don't know what else to do."

I turned to look at him and he took my hands.

"Maybe Sunday is just what you need. I know how you feel about God and all of the disappointments that you have endured but you have to admit that something is happening." I looked down and almost began to dismiss what he was saying. His grip on my hands tightened.

"I haven't made a big deal about the absence of God in our lives but you knew I grew up in church. I have to admit that my relationship with God didn't seem to be as solid as yours but even still, we need to think about Adam. He has obviously been positively affected by his exposure to God because of your mother. It's evident that he is interested in learning more. He has taught me, and if I am not mistaken, you, a few things. We need to provide him with the right environment." He paused and moved to stand by me with his back leaning against the sink. He released my hands and said solemnly, "I am not your father and I hope that Zion House is not in any way like New Light but history does have a habit of repeating itself. I'd hate to see Adam confused about what loving the Lord is really about. If we don't take an active role in teaching him, he may be misled and then wind up misrepresenting God. I know you don't want that. There are too many people doing that." He kissed me on the cheek. "You've never really stopped believing, Paige. I guess that I can understand why you have chosen to simply not care. Just promise me that you will hold onto what you heard about your mother. She will come out of it."

My head found a place on his shoulder. "Okay," I said, relenting, "for Adam." I exhaled audibly and turned to turn off the light over the sink. "Please go and see what Adam is up to. Maybe we can watch a movie together if he is not in the middle of a video game."

Why don't we go out and catch a movie? I hear that the kids are lovin' the newest Disney flick," he suggested.

"Sounds like a plan. I'm sure Adam would like that," I said. The dark cloud that hovered over me was showing signs of evaporating.

"Adam and I will check the schedule," he said as he walked out of the kitchen.

I turned out the light over the table and stood there for a moment with my elbows on the island. In the dark, I began to mentally prepare for church in two days. Count down...

"For you and Adam," I murmured into the darkness.

For some inane reason, I felt paralyzed Sunday morning. My psyche kept providing reasons why I shouldn't make good on my promise to Justin to attend Daniel's church. The arguments silently communicated ranged from the questionable color of the dress that I purchased for the occasion to service interrupting Adam's naptime. Pitiful, I know.

I had to actually mentally fight inwardly to rise out of the bed. I began mumbling, sounding quite crazy as I padded to the bathroom. I opened the door, to hear Justin in the shower. He was singing a song that I have never heard him sing. I immediately recognized it but I didn't know that he knew it.

"This is the day, this is the day that the Lord has made. I will rejoice and be glad in it," he sang.

I giggled to myself and quickly pulled back the shower curtain and began singing it with him. Justin was clearly off key but we continued to sing together. I held my nose playfully while looking at him, communicating that his singing stunk.

"Okay, okay. I know that I can't sing but I heard the song in my head and just started singing it," he said as he removed the shower head and rinsed the soap from his hairy chest. He moved the portable showerhead over his sculpted biceps and toned forearms. I slapped his firm behind, laughed and quickly closed the dusty rose colored shower curtain.

"I am going to get Adam ready, and then I'll take my shower," I announced, trying not to scream but wanting to make sure that he heard me over the running water. The water stopped and Justin stepped out of the shower. His body glistened. The beads of water looked like miniature diamonds on his washboard abdomen. He was breathtaking.

"Paige, get undressed and get in the shower now. I'll take care of Adam so that you can get yourself ready. I'd like to be on time. You know how much I despise latecomers and that counts double with church."

Because I wanted this to be a positive day, I grudgingly acquiesced. I could remember a time when that statement would have caused me to chuck the entire idea of attending church. The mere mentioning of being late for church would evoke memories of my childhood. The screaming and hollering that took place on Sunday mornings all in the name of getting to church on time was a painful memory that I couldn't shake. This morning however, I surprisingly decided not to take offense. Thankfully, I pressed Adam's outfit on Friday and put it out with the rest of his clothes for the coming week. The shoes that I purchase were perfect. He even liked them. Adam and Justin would be perfectly content to wear sneakers every day. Adam would have liked to wear his sandals but I thought the black lace-up shoes that were similar to his dad's would be a nice touch.

Justin nodded in the direction of the door to wordlessly communicate that I should get moving. I turned to leave the bathroom and quickly made the bed. When he exited the bathroom, I slipped into our walk-in closet to retrieve my orange wrap dress and matching sandals. The orange was a bit loud but it was mid-September so I thought that it would be okay.

Hearing Justin sing, although his rendition was in a key that only dogs could hear, had brightened my mood and the thoughts that clouded my head telling me that I shouldn't go to church were muted.

"I'll just rouse Adam to get him started and then I'll get in the shower," I said as I made my way down the hall toward Adam's room.

"Time to get up, baby," I sang. Adam stirred but didn't open his eyes. "Come on, sweet baby. We are going to church with Daddy today," I reminded him.

His eyes slowly opened and then a flash of recognition registered on his face. He seemed to pop up. His little brown toes hit the floor and heels followed. "Mornin', Mommy," he said finally, while rubbing his eyes. "Are we still going to church today?"

"Yes, we are going but you have to get moving so that we'll be on time," I said.

"Okay, I'll go brush my teeth. I'll brush them really good," he promised.

"Daddy will be in a minute to help you in the shower," I told him.

"Aw, Mommy, I can wash myself," he pouted.

"You are on your way but Dad just needs to make sure you get the important body parts, okay?"

"Okay, Mommy," he said with a lowering of his shoulders.

"Thanks, baby. I am going to get in the shower. Come get your dad when you are done with your teeth."

I headed back to my bathroom and began to shed my clothes, placing them into the adjacent hamper. I stepped into the running water after applying my face soap and rubbing it in. I usually let it sit to extract any dirt from my pores.

The water felt good. Although I was a bit nervous about going to Zion House after not attending a regular service for some time, I felt good that I could do something for Justin and Adam. I was hoping that I would get something out of it. Karlie seemed proud of me and she had even said so. "You may find out what is missing, Paige. Give it a chance."

I doubted that I'd be able receive anything from the service. After all, I'd heard it all before, or so I thought. I rinsed my face with warm water and enjoyed the cleansing of my body.

As we pulled up to the building, I lowered the sun visor so that I could check my make-up and hair prior to entering the church. Replacing the flap, I turned and looked at Justin. There was a hint of a smile emerging as he turned to me, looking as if he were pleased with what he saw.

"Mom, it looks like it's a small church," Adam observed.

"Yes, it is a small building but looks are sometimes deceiving," I answered.

"Daniel mentioned that it was a small congregation but every Sunday, they received new members," Justin informed.

We found a parking space not far from the entrance and I unlocked the car and exited. I let Adam out of the back seat and reached for his hand. We needed to cross the parking lot and there were a number of cars entering the parking area. Adam seemed very eager to reach to church so I held his hand tightly as we crossed the parking lot. As we drew nearer to the church, I could hear drums and an organ. I assumed the choir or praise team was singing already. We had arrived just in time.

At the entrance we were greeted by two pleasant looking African-American women.

"Good morning, welcome to Zion House." Their smiles seemed warm and genuine but I was uneasy about people and their masks. I played along, giving both them my best smile. The ladies embraced Justin and shook Adam's hand. The hug was not stiff or practiced. It felt sincere. We were provided with an offering envelope and shown to our seats. There were maybe about one hundred people in the congregation. I had expected more. I looked around nervously and placed my purse on the seat beside me. Almost everyone was standing and singing. They seemed to be praising God but again my pessimism kicked in and I decided that it wasn't a real show of worship and took my seat. To my surprise, Adam and Justin remained standing and started singing along. Adam knew the words of the song.

I mouthed the words. "I will dance, I will dance, I will dance like David danced." I didn't know the song as well as Adam knew it but I followed along.

Daniel approached the pulpit and sang along with the praise team. He looked better than the last time we saw him. At that time, his father had just died and it was rumored that his brother was going to be convicted of drug possession. The funeral was a sad one because the family said that the charges caused the subsequent heart attack that took Daniel's father's life. Daniel was in turmoil then. He knew that his brother had disappointed his mother and father and all of the people who believed in him.

Daniel had grown up with Justin in the church but moved away and had apparently found his way back. I guess that would explain his obvious physical metamorphosis. His skin looked a lot healthier and he seemed to have put on weight. I could tell that he was buff and had been working out. His light brown eyes had a certain clarity as he surveyed the congregation. He spotted Justin and smiled. The song came to an end and everyone took their seats.

"I'm so glad to be in the house of the Lord!" Daniel exclaimed, smiling and moving his arms enthusiastically. "I know how David felt when he said, 'I was glad when said unto to me let us go into the house of the Lord.'"

The congregation clapped emphatically in agreement with their pastor. "Amen" and "Yes, Lord" emitted from the mouths of the attendees.

"I know many of us didn't think that they would ever make it to see the inside of a church so if you have been delivered, you'd better act like you know and stand on your feet and give God some praise." The entire church stood to their feet. Thunderous praise filled the sanctuary.

Being the skeptic that I had become, I assessed the congregation. Their faces were sincere and the people seemed earnest in their praise.

"God has been too good for you to sit there and act like you are too good to praise Him. Think about where you would have been if it had not been for God's grace and His love. Here's the kicker." He paused and looked around smiling while jumping up and down. "We didn't even deserve His grace or his love not to mention Jesus dying on the cross for us. He took on the sins that were yet to be committed, dragged them with him to the cross and buried them in the tomb with him. When he rose, our slate had been wiped clean. All we have to do is believe and accept Him as our Savior and Lord." He moved to the far side of the church as if to speak to that part of the house specifically. "To just know that we have life and life more abundantly should make you jump out of your seat and praise the Lord." The organ was off and running and the place was a cacophony of worship.

I'd have to give it to Daniel; he really knew how to work the crowd and get them ready to praise God.

"You know what, church?" he said. "I am not here to get you pumped because if you know what God has done in your life you should come to church pumped to receive what thus saith the Lord. If you want to receive your blessing from the word that will come forth you'd better get your own Jesus pom-poms out and start giving Him the praise because He alone is worthy."

It was as if someone had whispered my thoughts into Daniel's ears. I felt my face begin to get warm.

Once the praise and worship had concluded, the church service continued. The announcements were made and then any other announcements that Daniel wanted to communicate to the congregation were provided.

"Do we have any visitors in the house today?" Daniel inquired.

I turned to Justin and he nodded and we all stood to our feet, smiling. One of the ladies that greeted us from the front door found her way to us and provided us with a welcome packet and hugged me again.

"Praise God," Daniel said. "My buddy from back in the day is visiting us today with his lovely wife and son. I am so glad to see you today, Justin and Paige."

He stopped and looked around the congregation for any other first-time visitors. Because there weren't any others, he turned back to Justin and I and said, "Again, we praise God for you today and ask that you not make this visit your last. You may be seated." He turned to the organist and he began to play an interlude as the ushers approached the pulpit and gathered the buckets. *Offering time,* I surmised silently.

"Church, it is offering time. We know that in the Word it is our responsibility to tithe. Please complete the offering envelope."

Daniel took a few steps back so that he could stand behind the glass podium. I left the offering to Justin. He completed the envelope and put the check inside. I made a mental note to ask him how much we gave. I looked down at Adam who sat between Justin and me. He looked so handsome in his white oxford shirt with blue striped tie and matching blue khakis. His hair was freshly cut. I placed my arm around him and hugged him to my breast. He looked up and smiled.

"Mommy, this church is better than Grandma's." I nodded in agreement. "Will I be able to learn with the other children?"

I shrugged my shoulders but at that moment, an attractive honey-colored woman wearing a peach linen pant suit announced that the children were dismissed for Children's Church. Adam's face lit up. My eyes found Justin's to get his take on it. I was a bit apprehensive but I thought I'd let Justin make this call as well. I knew Adam wanted to participate and didn't want to be the one to burst his bubble. Justin nodded his approval. Adam grabbed my hand and he practically pulled me to my feet. He led me out of the aisle. I followed the other kids to the back and made inquiries as to where Adam would be placed. I quickly got him settled while meeting the teacher. She seemed competent enough, I thought.

I returned to my seat and moved over one chair to sit closer to Justin. I appraised the setting and décor of the church. The walls were painted a salmon color. The large windows used their vertical blinds to welcome the September sun as it spread its light to every angle of the spacious room. Because the windows surrounded the room, the sheer lavender valances that swung from one end of each window to the other acted as eyelids. There were beautiful although artificial bouquets of flowers at the lip of the raised pulpit. The two outside seats were regal in purple with hints of gold but not overly ostentatious. The glass podium sat in front of the three high-backed chairs. They could have passed for mini thrones. The pews had purple cushions with flecks of gold and the back was newly shined maple wood with a small piece of the same cushion in the middle of the wooded area for one's back.

That was a nice touch, I thought. The carpet matched the gold in the pews and also the pulpit chairs. There was a large cross hanging behind the pulpit that had a violet hue. Below the cross, the light gray baptismal pool was encased in glass. I decided that it was a comfortable place to worship and not too over-the-top. Compared to the sanctuaries that I had seen, Zion House was quite modest.

Daniel was standing in front of the pulpit when I returned my attention to the service. He was holding what looked like a well-worn bible.

"Okay, are we ready to be fed?" he asked, scanning the church expectantly. Clearly this question was not rhetorical because he held his hand to his ear to indicate that we needed to respond. There was a resounding "yes" from the congregation.

"Alright, let's see what God has to say to us today."

Daniel turned and headed to the podium and opened his bible. As I prepared myself to receive the word, my mind drifted to Mom and how happy she would be to know that I was sitting in a church, knowing that it wasn't a holiday or a special occasion would really make her day. Maybe her prayers were being answered right now. I still didn't understand what was going on with her. A wave of frustration hit me. Why was it taking so long for her to come back to us? I didn't know if I could be patient for much longer. Doubt once again entered my thoughts. *Why did I always fall for the Jesus okie-dokie?* I thought to myself. I knew that I had distanced myself from Him so why would He even bother speak to me? No, I decided angrily, it was not the Spirit of God speaking to me. Wishful thinking just manifested itself with the help of my familiarity with the bible. I raised my head to face the pulpit, quickly cementing my decision to not be swayed by anything and felt a nudge.

As if reading my thoughts, Justin turned to me. His face was expressionless. He then quickly turned away. It wasn't very often that I couldn't read him.

How do you explain the other verses and words being spoken to your heart, Paige?

Oh my goodness, there it was again. I looked at Justin again and he seemed to be engrossed in what Daniel was saying.

"Let's go to Matthew, the seventh chapter and the twenty-first and twenty-second verses. We will use this as our starting point scripture. Say 'amen' when you have it."

To my surprise Justin revealed my old bible and started flipping the pages. The entire church was filled with the sounds of pages quickly moving. Once locating the scripture, Justin said amen. I smiled at his eagerness to participate in the service. I began to once again become encouraged. I felt like a seesaw. One minute I was up and the next I was down. I had contracted the children of Israel virus.

"Let us read this aloud. Oh and forgive me, add on the twenty-third verse because that is the clincher," he said.

"'Not everyone that saith unto me Lord, Lord, shall enter in into the kingdom of heaven; but he that doeth the will of my Father which is in heaven. Many will say to me in that day, Lord, Lord, have we not prophesied in thy name? And in thy name cast out devils? And in thy name done many wonderful works? And I will then profess unto them, I never knew you, depart from me, ye that work iniquity.'"

"Church, everyone who says that they are a Christian is not necessarily a Christian. There are too many of us who think just because they can cut a good step and shout hallelujah that they are on their way to heaven. Saints of God, I have news for ya. That is not the way it works."

My mouth dropped open and I sat back in my seat. Words could not express how I felt at that moment. I stared at Daniel and wanted to absorb everything that would come out of Daniel's mouth. I even caught myself saying "amen." He took us to scripture after scripture that supported the crux of his message. It was made abundantly clear biblically that we shouldn't look to man or put our trust in man but only in God.

Hadn't Mom been trying to tell me that same thing?

A passage that I decided to commit to memory was Psalms 118:8. "It is better to trust in the Lord than to put confidence in man." He talked about the present-day Pharisees and I almost fell out of my seat. Daniel directed the congregation to Matthew 23:14. *"Woe unto you scribes and Pharisees, hypocrites for ye devour women's houses and for pretence make long prayer, therefore receive greater damnation."* Although I knew all of this in some way, seeing it in the bible made it so much more clear. Daniel was certainly making it plain. All through the sermon, he continued to make the point that although many of us feel that these people are getting away with making Christianity a charade, we had to trust God. We had to believe that God was going to handle the people who have done wrong and performed deeds that were not Christ-like without repenting and asking forgiveness from the recipients of their evil doings. We can't allow them to keep us from being the Christians that we need to be. We should not let them cause us to stumble.

As he said these words, I thought of all the people that were still "playing with God" and wondered if they had any idea that they were headed for a lot of trouble. I thought of my dad and the many people that I had seen in action and began to feel pity for them. I had a decision to make. Was I going to let them dictate my relationship with God?

Based upon on what Daniel showed us in scripture, if we were willing and obedient, we would have all that we needed through Christ Jesus. His promises to the true Christians were all through the bible.

"I can feel that some of you have been battling with feelings that only God can help you defeat," Daniel said. "You have to let go of whatever has you bound. Someone who claimed to be a Christian has hurt you or misled you and caused you to risk you heavenly home. Please don't let anyone, least of all a fake Christian, come between you and Jesus. You will lose out every time and the devil will have won."

He made a few more statements and closed. I was in awe of the revelation that I received during the sermon. I had no idea that it was going to be so applicable to my life. As we stood for the altar call, I felt a tap on my shoulder. Justin was making his way past me. He squeezed my hand and continued to move toward the aisle. It became apparent to me that he wanted me to go with him. Fear and apprehension gripped me and I released his hand. His eyes filled with disappointment but he kept going. When he reached the front of the sanctuary, he was embraced warmly by Daniel. I, on the other hand, felt betrayed. I wasn't exactly angry at Justin but I thought that we should have talked about it first.

The choir began to sing a song that also seemed speak to me as well. What was this? Was I on Jesus' radar today?

The words, "Come back to your first love," were so true. Jesus was my first love but I couldn't shake the feelings of apprehension. I needed time to think about it. The choir continued to sing, "God will show you His will if you listen."

"Jesus can fill any void in your life. Some of you already know that Jesus is the answer but have been running from Him for a while now. Stop running from Him and run to Him. He can complete you like nothing and no one else can. You know who you are. Just admit to yourself that you need Jesus. Do that and He will make your decision to connect or reconnect with him easier."

I knew that I needed Him in my life.

I knew that the truth had just been revealed to me. I became repentant at that moment.

I was sorry for denying this need for so long.

"I need you, Jesus, but help me to be real. If I can't be real then I don't want to have any part of this. I am sorry, restore me."

Wiping unrealized tears from my cheeks, I excused myself and made my way to the ladies' restroom.

Chapter 18

The ride home was weird. The whole world seemed to be mute as we made our way back to our house.

Upon entering the house, the gift of noise returned. Adam was pumped about going back to Zion House and Justin was pumped about being part of a church family again and actually rededicating his life to Christ. I, on the other hand, knowing in my heart that Jesus was the missing piece in my life, remained silent. I didn't know what to say and couldn't determine honestly if I had a right to say anything.

I directed Adam to go to his room and change his clothes. I told him that I'd be up to help him hang them up.

"Okay, Mommy." He looked at me quizzically. "Are you okay? You are talking awfully soft. Are you hurt?"

"No, baby, Mommy is fine," I responded to him with a faint smile. "Just go on upstairs and I'll be there in a minute."

Adam shrugged his shoulders and scampered up the stairs to his room. I kicked off my sandals and went into the kitchen to find something to eat. The idea came to me in the car that Justin and Daniel should go out for dinner by themselves. This would give them an opportunity to catch up from the male perspective.

"Are you changing clothes for dinner?" Justin asked as he entered the kitchen noticing that I had untied my wrap dress and allowed it to hang open loosely.

"You know, I think that you and Daniel should go out this evening. Just the two of you," I said, trying to hold in my emotions. My back was to him so he couldn't see my face.

"Okay, Paige, out with it," he said.

Dagnibit, I thought. I didn't want to discuss it. My mind was too clouded.

I turned to find him sitting at the kitchen table with one leg folded in a ninety-degree angle over his other knee. He looked at me with a little frustration shrouding his countenance.

He has the audacity to be frustrated with me? I thought to myself.

I pictured him once again sauntering up to the pulpit without a thought as to how this decision would affect me. I didn't say anything for a minute or two.

He exhaled loudly and I decided that we might as well have it out now.

"How could you go to the altar without talking it over with me, Justin?" I said, not caring if I sounded a little hurt.

"Paige, there wasn't any time to think about how it was going to affect anyone. I only knew that I had a decision to make and it had to do with my soul, not yours. I am not going to join the church without you but I did dedicate my life once again to Jesus Christ. It has been tugging at me for some time now and I couldn't wait any longer. If it is any consolation, you helped me to do what I needed to do," he confessed.

"Oh? How so?" I couldn't wait to hear this.

"You reminded me of the story of Samuel and how he heard the voice of the Lord. He didn't know who it was. When the prophet Eli told him to answer it the next time he heard it, Samuel did. You have been lucky enough to continue to hear from the Lord but yet you deny Him. He continues to talk to you. When you shared that with me, it was my wake-up call. I have to be ready to answer the Lord when He calls me. I want to be unafraid to answer Him. I want to be like Samuel ready to do what the Lord wants me to do."

He searched my face for understanding.

I did understand but I never knew he felt this way. "I want a relationship with Jesus," he said in an effort to allow his words to sink into me. "I heard His voice today."

"How could I have been so blind?" I said quietly. I found a chair and slowly lowered my body into it. "Why didn't you ever tell me about this before?" I asked, feeling ashamed.

"You know why," he said.

I could see that he didn't want to point the finger back at me.

"If I would have told you, you would have probably talked me out of it by talking about the many hypocrites that you've dealt with in the past and how Jesus is not this and not that."

He stood up and walked over to the island in the kitchen and leaned against it. "The distance that you have kept from Jesus has kept all of us from Him. Until recently, it didn't seem like you were going to let me any closer to you, either. I know you didn't mean to do it but..."

I had done exactly what Daniel said. My behavior, whether intentional or not, had kept others from knowing Christ. My husband and son could have been the casualties of the war that I was having with God. I was trying so hard not to be a hypocrite and not to be one of the ones that misrepresented Christ. In actuality, I was far worse. I knew the right way and kept my family from reaping the rewards of knowing God.

"I am so sorry, honey. I didn't mean to," I said softly, trying to stop the tears from flowing.

"I know you didn't mean to, you were wrestling feelings of your own and couldn't see what you were doing," he said as he walked around the island to fold me in his arms.

"I am happy for you, Justin. I want you to have a connection with God. Just don't judge me too harshly."

I could feel him laugh softly and he held me tighter.

Adam walked into the kitchen with a frightened look on his face when he saw the streaks of tears on my face.

"I knew something was wrong. Mommy, what is the matter?" he asked and hugged my waist.

"Mommy is fine or at least I will be." I looked at Justin and he nodded.

"If you promise that you'll be okay, can I go over to James' house to play video games this afternoon? He invited me over," Adam asked, forgetting that he was once concerned about my emotional status.

"I'll call Mrs. Donnelly and if she is okay with it, you can go," I said, releasing myself from Justin's embrace. I patted Adam's head and walked over to the phone.

As I reached for the cordless phone to dial Mrs. Donnelly's number, it rang. Looking at the caller ID displayed on the window, I recognized the hospital's number. I braced myself and said, "Hello?"

"Paige, get to the hospital as soon as you can. Mom has just regained consciousness and is asking to see all of us."

It was Celia. She sounded if she were laughing and crying at the same time.

I heard myself tell her that I was going to drop off Adam at a friend's house and make my way over. I hung up and quickly found a place to sit down. I placed my hands on the table to steady them. Adam and Justin looked at me expectantly but didn't dare utter a word to try and hasten my explanation of the call. I was silent for was moment and then lifted my head with a smile that had to be one hundred watts.

"Mom is out of the coma!" I shouted.

"Thank you, Jesus," both of my men said in unison.

This surprised me but, then again, it somehow didn't. I didn't linger on their response for too long.

We decided that Adam would go to James' house for the afternoon and that I'd pick him up after my visit with Mom. Justin would go to dinner with Daniel and we'd all meet back at the house later.

I called Mrs. Donnelly to confirm that it would be okay. She was a responsible and no-nonsense Mom like myself. I changed my clothes, made a quick lunch for Justin and Adam and was out of the door.

Chapter 19

It was so good seeing Mom sitting up in bed and conversing. As I sat at her bedside in amazement, I held her hand tightly, being careful not to squeeze it too hard

"Mom, Paige said that you wouldn't die and that you would come out of it," Celia revealed as she looked back at me with grateful eyes.

Although her voice was soft, Mom's voice had a certain strength that was beneath her words. "Is that true, Paige?"

She looked at me with an interesting stare.

I couldn't quite place the expression. It looked as if she knew that I was the one that kept the family believing but wasn't sure if I really believed it. It was weird.

I blinked and turned my head to look at Loni and then said, "I just heard it in my heart. It was as simple as that, Mom," I breathed. I now wanted to take the spotlight off of me and return it to Mom.

"I feel so blessed to have my family in my presence. God is truly worthy to be praised," Mom said.

"Amen," my father said as he exited the bathroom and stood on the other side of Mom's bed.

In that split second, I could feel myself stiffen. I stood to my feet to offer Darlene my seat. Mom did not let go of my hand.

"You must forgive, Paige," Mom whispered.

"I am working on it, Mom." I kissed her on the cheek.

She released my hand and looked up at Dad and placed my hand in his. He held onto it and out of respect her, I didn't wrench it away.

"Paige," my dad said, "no more hypocrisy."

I looked away. I've heard all of this before.

"I am sorry for everything," he said.

"Dad, Mom is tired. Do we really need to go into everything now?" I asked not ready to hear his apologies.

"Yes, baby, you need to hear it all now," Mom said.

I removed my hand from Dad's hand walked around toward the end of the bed to let Darlene sit down. "If this is what you both want, we are all here," I said extending my hand in the direction of Loni, Tyler, Blue and Celia.

Dad rose to stand squarely on his feet. "I don't think that I ever talked about my upbringing and I guess that was done on purpose because it wasn't one that I want to remember. My father, although revered in the county, was a hard man. This was an oddity as he was a black man. He was known because of his involvement in the community. In those days, the community was essentially the church."

He looked at Mom and she nodded as if encouraging him to continue.

"My father and mother were not in love, I don't think that they ever loved each other. I learned that my father had gotten my mother pregnant with me and her father forced her to marry him. He was not happy about this union and as a result, she suffered for it. He seemed not to care about me or my mother. This became worse as the years progressed and James and Quinton came along. My father was abusive in action and in words to both myself and Mother. When he learned that he would get more respect by being in the church, he really became absent from our lives. What I mean to say is that we would attend church together and put on a good show when we were out in the street just in case someone he knew was around but when we were home he was a different person, always angry and bitter. He would give Mother just enough money to by food and maybe we'd get a suit of clothes two times a year. He was emotionally and physically absent, always saying that he had church work. Sometimes he'd be gone for weeks. When I was a child, I thought it was how every other family behaved. As I got older, it became frighteningly clear that it wasn't the norm. All the while my father would be at church acting like the best father on earth. Praying, singing and even giving speeches." Dad breathed and his shoulders slumped just a little.

"I know that you may be thinking that I turned into him and you are right, I did. Quinton and James somehow learned the lesson and as soon as they finished school, they left home. When they became settled, they both sent for Mother. She was all too happy to join them. She was tired of living in a house with dirt floors and cooking over a fireplace. All of my father's women were living in better houses than my own mother. I tried to leave but the spirit of my father attached itself to me and I couldn't shake loose until I met your mother. I told myself that I would be a better man. I failed. The worst part of it was that I was blessed to have daughters. I didn't know how to show you how much I loved you. I was unable to lavish my girls with the love I didn't receive. Making matters worse, I had found the woman of my dreams and all I did was constantly disappoint her, looking for something that I had all the while." Mom reached up and touched Dad's hand.

"Paige, you received so much of that anger. I don't why you did....but you made me look at myself and then I would see Father in me. I'd become angry and take my anger out on you more so than your sisters. You were so headstrong and independent for a baby child. You didn't deserve it. You were a good daughter."

His eyes fell on Celia, Loni and Darlene. "You all were good children in spite of me being a horrible example of a father. I am so glad that you have chosen husbands who will give you the love and treat you like the queens that you are." He began to cry. His shoulders shook and he leaned over the bed rail to embrace Mom. "You didn't deserve to be treated the way you were. You are a saint and the only woman that I have ever loved. I love you, Livie. I hope that you have always known that."

Mom nodded and a tears escaped her eyes as well.

Darlene stood up and went over to Dad and put her arms around him.

I stood absolutely still.

"I just don't understand," I said, not really moved by his tearful display or his story. "If you knew that you were acting like Granddad, why didn't you seek help or seek out the Lord earnestly and not continue to be fake or misrepresent him? Do you know how many people you have misdirected and turned away from Christ because of your behavior?" I spewed angrily.

He looked at me with repented eyes. "Paige, I don't know why. I know that you have stayed away because of me. I don't know if I'll ever be able to make it up to you but I am going to try to make it up to all of you—"

"That's not good enough!" I screamed.

Loni touched my arm to calm me.

"Your mother and I have sought the Lord on this and I have resigned from the deacon board."

"Well, it's about time," I released cruelly.

"Paige," Mother said. "I have to take some of the blame. I could have left your father when I found out about his cheating and other behavior especially his physical attacks on my children but I lied to myself and said that it was simply discipline. I decided to stay because it was what I felt the Lord would have me do. I know you remember the long trips out of town that we took without your dad. Think hard about it. Try and remember. Remember the one after that Thanksgiving?"

I thought about it and I remembered that Dad never said anything or even came close to laying a hand on me or my sisters after we arrived home in the new year following that catastrophe. We were gone at least a month.

"I knew that your father had a troubled childhood but I also knew that he needed love and understanding. I knew that God would have His way with him. I just had to trust and wait. Since you girls have been gone your father is the most gentle and loving man. He loves the Lord and has not been an active deacon for the last year. He wants to work on his walk with God. People still don't want to believe it but it is true. He doesn't even want to participate on the church advisory board."

"It was time that I had to come to grips with what kind of man I was and focus on the kind of man I want my children and grandchildren to remember and be proud of. Most importantly, I am striving to be the man that God wants me to be."

He cleared his voice and I could hear the phlegm that had made its way to his throat. I was doubly repulsed.

My heart was hardened. "The Pharaoh Complex" is what Karlie called it.

"Paige, I know that you don't let Adam stay overnight at our house because of me and I understand. I hope that I will someday gain your trust," Dad said. His eyes set on me. "Loni is about to have one of her own and I want to be allowed to be a true granddad to my second grandchild."

This is too much, I thought. *Dad quit the deacon board and his position on the church advisory board?* Black men craved a title in the church. Well, at least most of the older ones. I was scared to believe that he was trying to change.

"Please let me try…" Dad said in a voice that was stitched with sincerity.

I looked at my watch and noticed that it was almost seven o'clock. I had to get home. Mrs. Donnelly said that she would feed Adam but I needed to go and get ready for the week. All of this was a lot to take in one sitting.

"All of this is enlightening but I have to get going. Adam has camp tomorrow and I have to get ready for the work week," I said, gathering my purse and walking toward Mom to give her a kiss.

"I am so grateful that you are with us and that you are going to be okay. I love you."

"Paige, I know that something is going on with you," Mom said perceptively. I was beginning to believe that she could read my thoughts.

"You have to let go so that God can complete you. Only He can. You can't blame others for what's missing in your life. You have the opportunity to get all that God has for you. Don't miss it." She smiled and blew me a kiss. Her lips parted but she closed them as if deciding not to say anything. I stared at her for a moment.

"Mom, when you were unconscious, you were moving your lips as if you were talking but you didn't utter a sound. We all thought that it was a good sign and that you were trying to come back to us but when it stopped, I have to admit that I became a bit scared."

I didn't know if I was making any sense but I had to know what that was all about and only she would have the answer.

She reached for me and I drew closer to her. Giving Dad a quick glance, he moved toward the back of the room.

"When I was unconscious I had the most wonderful encounter." She smiled as she began the recall her experience. "I knew that I was dreaming but it was so very real to me. I was praying at the feet of the Lord. I was asking him to restore my family. I asked him not to take me until my family was a loving unit. He told me that he was working on you and that your heart was very heavy." Her expression as she recounted the event was dreamlike.

She turned to face me and her eye became glassy. "The prayers of the righteous availeth much," she whispered. "I know that you may have thought that was placed on your heart for the people that were praying for me but I was soliciting God's mercy for you. I do believe that my prayers will avail."

"Mom, no…" I couldn't believe what she was saying. I held onto the railing of the bed to help me stand. Only Mom. She was petitioning God in Jesus' name even while unconscious?!

Words escaped me as I then placed my hands delicately on each side of her face and bore into her with my eyes. I was searching for the answer that God had given her. I wasn't entirely sure that I believed one hundred percent of her story but her eyes didn't waver. I knew that she believed what she was telling me.

"Thank you, Mom," I said as my hands fell from her face. No other words were necessary. I guess we would have to wait and see.

Stunned and a little off-balance, I turned to walk toward the door.

Dad stopped me and said earnestly, "Paige, I know we have a long way to go but think about what was been said today." His eyes glistened with unspent tears.

Unaware of the source, anger swirled inside of me like a tornado.

How could God restore this family? Restore means to repair. We were never a family. Rebellion and defiance clouded my sight. I know it may have seemed ungrateful but there were issues yet to be resolved.

"You know what you have done to not only me but Mom and countless others. How should I feel right now?" I challenged, wanting him to really comprehend the gravity of the pain that he had caused.

For if ye forgive men their trespasses, your heavenly Father will also forgive you. But if you forgive not men their trespasses, neither will your Father forgive your trespasses.

I really didn't need to hear that, I responded to my inner witness inaudibly.

I couldn't forget what Daniel said today. I couldn't let anyone keep me from reconnecting with the Lord. How was I going to accomplish that with my feelings resembling a pendulum?

Deciding to place the events of the last hour in back of my mind, I resigned myself to the task of focusing on the impending work week and how I was going to make it through without losing it.

"Paige, I am not certain that I was clear in regard to our direction for the Rosenfeld account but allow me to take this opportunity to clarify our plan of action for the enrollment process as the client would like to see it," Myra explained during our conference call. "It is important that we enroll as many employees as possible into the new plan. Although the main decision-maker has changed his mind and has communicated that the HMO plan will be his health plan of choice, he did not want to stop the process that we have set in motion."

I was tiring of her empty soliloquies about how we needed to appease the client at all cost. It was clear that she wanted to earn as much money as she could on commission and wanted a substantial amount of enrollments. I just wished she would take over the whole process. My other accounts were coming along smoothly. This was the only one that seemed to be an issue. There always had to be one, I guessed. The requests for enrollment meetings and benefit seminars had begun and if I was going to get some assistance with my accounts that had locations across the country, it was only right that I assist with the incoming meeting requests. Services issues involving claims and eligibility discrepancies could be left to my claims consultants and eligibility reps. They knew how to reach me when the traveling began.

"Paige, are you with me?" Myra asked.

"Certainly, Myra," I said without hearing all of what Myra had just stated.

"I understand that you are unable to do all the meetings but it is imperative that you conduct the meetings that are in the corporate locations," Myra confirmed.

I decided not to object and allow my schedule to dictate my availability. I know that I was not going to be able to attend all of the corporate meetings but didn't have the energy to ignite any fires during this call.

"I'll consult my schedule. I know that it is becoming quite booked," I said, inferring that we'd better look at others avenues to ensure that representatives were available should I not be able to be present. "I have to jump off this call as I have to prepare for another one in ten minutes. If there is anything else that I need to do, please simply e-mail me," I said in my syrupy sweet voice. "Have a good day, all."

Chapter 20

The month of September quickly became a memory and October was proving to be even crazier than predicted. I really despised wasting my time on conference calls. Meetings with Myra and the Rosenfeld team were beginning to get on my nerves. The client had finally sent me their proposed times and dates for their enrollment meetings and after much prodding by myself and Myra, the schedule was finally solidified. Thankfully, my other accounts sent over their schedules two weeks prior and the early bird always got the worm. My calendar became populated so fast that I couldn't even believe it. I'd be doing a lot of overnight travel. Fortunately, I liked visiting the NY Solutions account and the others weren't too bad. Rosenfeld had to be happy with what I could provide. I was successful in talking some of the Rosenfeld corporate locations into conference call enrollment meetings. I could tell that Myra was not pleased with that suggestion but the client loved it and ate it up. I could certainly facilitate those.

After e-mailing my availability to the client and sending out counterpart requests to cover and assist in presenting to Rosenfeld at their company locations, I signed off and closed my laptop. Although some time has passed since my conversation with June, I still felt that something was up but couldn't put my finger on it. Another meeting with the client was scheduled next Monday. We had been successful in getting their sign-off on the presentation and all of the enrollment materials had been sent to the client. They communicated that their employees had received them and were ready to attend the meetings with questions. Most seemed interested because the cost was significantly lower for an employee and family if they chose the new offering plan. We were unable to increase the HMO rate very much but the HRA option was competitive.

As I descended the stairs, I could smell the baked chicken in the oven. I opened the oven to baste it to ensure that it wouldn't become dry. String beans and Zatarain's Carribean rice would set the dinner off quite nicely. Mom and Dad were coming over for dinner and I was just happy to be hosting them. Mom was getting around really well and thought it would be a good idea for them to join us for a Friday evening dinner. Justin was due home any minute with Adam, which helped me out a great deal. He and Adam continued to surprise me with their unending interest in the bible. Justin had been spending a great deal of time with Daniel. He helped Daniel research scriptures for his weekly sermons and I really could see his growth. Sometimes I felt tremors of guilt when I thought of how my issues almost kept him from what had made such a difference in his life. I was coming along too. We just hadn't decided on becoming members. I knew that I had to make a decision because Justin had mentioned it almost every day. Knowing that the absence of Christ was the cause of my empty feelings had been made real to me but like a junkie who knew that he should enter rehab for the help that was desperately needed, I was sorely opposed to reconnecting myself with God by way of Christian fellowship. I just wanted to worship God in the privacy of my own home. I kept telling myself that I had to think it through. I had to be ready to immerse myself in the life. Too much had happened.

I found comfort in knowing that I could hear that still small voice that let me know that God loved me and waited for me to come to the realization that I would need to fellowship with other Christians sooner or later.

The doorbell chimed as I checked the clock over the range. It read 5:30 p.m. They were early and the men hadn't come home yet. I was greeted by a bouquet of flowers.

I smiled and my voice oozed sexiness. "Thanks, sailor. You'd better get in here before my husband comes home. He is quite jealous."

I winked in Adam's direction, spotting him behind the coral and yellow mums in the flower bed.

"Hey, woman!" Justin said and feigned a wounded expression.

"Oh! It's you?!" I shouted, laughing at him. "Thanks for the flowers, baby. Come on in, Mom and Dad should be here any minute."

As soon as the men washed up for dinner and changed their clothes, the doorbell rang again.

"Justin, can you get it. I am putting dinner on the table," I yelled, making my way to the dining room with the chicken.

It smelled great. The meal looked wonderful with everything situated on the table.

"Hi, Paige," Mom said as she placed the chocolate cake on the island in the kitchen.

"Hi, Mom, you look great." She was wearing a cranberry pantsuit that seemed to shimmer against her beautiful Indian summer skin. Her shiny onyx hair was pulled back into a bun at the nape of her neck.

"This is your cake, right? Don't play, Mom," I said with a look of exaggerated seriousness.

"Now you know that I wouldn't bring anything but the best to your house," she said and playfully slapped my behind. "Don't let me have to get with you."

We laughed. It was so good to laugh with her. She was really still here with me. I had so much to be thankful for.

Adam entered the kitchen in Dad's arms and I tried my best to greet Dad in a cheerful manner.

"Boy, get down. You grandfather can't always carry you. You are too big for that," I said to Adam with a frown on my face.

"It's okay, Paige, I picked him up," Dad said, not looking at me but staring at Adam as if he was honored to be carrying him.

"Alright," I said, putting an end to the exchange.

"Let's eat," Justin said, rubbing his hands. "Everything smells so good."

We walked into the dining room after all had washed their hands and gathered around the table, we asked the blessing over the food. I nodded at Justin. This was his house and I wanted him to pray.

Memories of Dad jumping in to pray at every family event came to my mind. We would stand for what seemed like a full thirty minutes. No way, not today.

Forgive and forget, Paige...

"Father God, we just thank you for your love. We thank you for your constant mercy. You have allowed us to gather again to partake of a meal that You have made possible. We ask for continued health and prosperity. Bless us in each of our lives. Touch us, Lord, and cleanse us as only you can. Let us follow your example. Thank you for the chef that prepared this meal and continue to reveal yourself in not only her life but in all of our lives. Let the food we consume nourish our bodies but let us continue to look to You for spiritual nourishment. We thank you and count in all joy in Jesus' name, Amen."

I knew that Justin was talking about me and at that moment I simply decided to let it go and let the Lord help me to move forward. He would continue to help me to forgive.

The dinner was the best one that I hosted in a long while. We all laughed and I even had a sidebar conversation with Dad. That had to be God.

"It's Friday night, Paige. Why don't you and Justin go out for a nice dinner and let Adam come over and spend the night with me and your father," Mom suggested. She didn't let me avert her gaze but stared into me for an answer.

This was the test.

I was finally able to turn to look at Justin and he smiled with a nod. "Okay, but we'll get him first thing in the morning," I said with audible apprehension.

After cake and coffee, Adam ran upstairs with my dad and Justin to gather what he needed for his overnight adventure.

"Thank you, Paige. You don't know what this means to your father," Mom said.

I nodded, not wanting anything sarcastic to escape my lips.

"We'll have a good time and he'll be in bed by 9:30 p.m. Is that okay?"

"That's fine, Mom," I said. "Please keep watch over my baby."

"I will. I promise," she pledged; her smile was one of assurance.

As I walked my parents and Adam to the car, I hugged my baby boy and said a prayer of protection over my child. It seemed that I now prayed quite often. I realized that I wanted to communicate with God and looked forward to hearing from Him.

Adam was so excited. He smiled brightly and allowed Dad to place the seatbelt around him securely. Crazily, Dad seemed even more excited than Adam.

I hugged Mom. I shocked myself and hugged Dad too.

As I walked back up the walk toward the house, I thought about my visit to my old church, New Light, last Sunday. I think that it was just what I needed to place all of the bad and hurt feelings to rest. Upon entering the sanctuary that seemed not to have changed throughout the years, except for the new pews, my chest began to tighten as my mind turned back the clock. I thought of all the people who displayed such disrespect for God and how I let that distance me from the only person who would never let me down. It was Youth Sunday and the young people of the church were in charge of the service. I enjoyed the new worship service and how the participants seemed to be earnest in their praise.

Was there a difference or was it me that was different? I thought.

They seemed stronger than I remembered because they were more familiar and grounded in the word of God. At least they wouldn't be fooled into thinking that the way I did.

I was amused when Mom and Dad entered the church and sat in the pews toward the back. I was so used to Dad sitting in the front row. He seemed a little humble in his greetings to others as he settled into his seat. Mom was smiling as she turned to see me sitting on the other side of the sanctuary.

The Youth Choir began to sing, and it reminded me of the many Sundays that I sang in the choir loft looking out into to congregation. The song, "Here I Am to Worship" by Israel and New Breed was being sung and heard and the words tugged at my heart. "I'll never know how much it cost, to see my sin up on the cross."

In that moment, I knew that I had to take some accountability for my relationship or lack thereof with God. His word had always been there and He, thankfully, never changed. I couldn't blame the phonies in the church, my dad or my mom for the issues that I had with Christ. I couldn't even blame God because He warned us consistently about wolves in sheep's clothing. It was all me. I was always the one holding back. I didn't seek His counsel by accessing His word.

Why couldn't I have seen this? Why didn't I seek out God when I was confused?

When I needed wisdom, the book of James clearly said to simply ask the Lord. Why hadn't I? He died on the cross for me. He wouldn't have done that and then leave me without direction or guidance. That is what His Word was for.

Many are the plans in a man's heart but it is the Lord's purpose that prevails.

I understood what was being said to my heart.

Regardless of what the liars and cheats try to accomplish, God's plan will win out. He is always victorious and so am I, I thought.

I was so unworthy and ashamed of my unnecessary ignorance.

The choir continued to sing and I became even more grateful. Through it all, He still loved me. As much as I fought and denied Him, He didn't give up on me. I was thankful that I was led here on this Sunday. Songs always seemed to minister to me and this song had opened the floodgates to my understanding.

As I opened my mouth to praise God, I knew immediately that I had been restored.

The spirit whispered to my heart: *I will seek that was lost and bring again which was driven away.*

I began to sing the song with renewed confidence. Deacon Matthews turned and saw me standing in my row, lifting up holy hands and singing. He made his way over to me.

"I can still recognize your voice, Paige. Come on up and sing." His eyes were warm and genuine.

Without reservation, I followed him to the front of the church. I stood behind the microphone and let the words flow from my mouth in song. It was as if I had never stopped singing.

Chapter 21

There I was standing in the church that I promised that I would never return to, fully realizing and accepting my own faults and asking the Lord to forgive me so that I could have the relationship with Him that I was meant to have.

Jesus, I said to myself, as I stood at the microphone, you sure do have a sense of humor.

I smiled and surveyed my surroundings. Strangely enough, I finally appreciated all that I had witnessed. It certainly made me understand that I had to be real for Christ if no one else was.

But my righteous ones will live by their faith.

The choir ended the song and the church stood to their feet. Obediently, I began to simply praise the Lord. I opened my mouth to audibly acknowledge His greatness and how awesome He was. I thanked Him and thanked Him and thanked Him. I was made to praise the Lord.

After church, I made my way over to the where my parents were standing. They were obviously happy to see me there. Unfortunately, I decided to visit alone. Justin and Adam went to Zion House.

"My heart leaped when you started singing, Paige," Mom said, her eyes sparkling. "I have prayed to hear your voice again." She looked beautiful in her beige suit and matching wide-brimmed hat.

"I just thought I needed to stop in and see how you were and then I was asked to sing. I am trying to be obedient," I said.

"You were wonderful," Dad said with a genuine smile. "How are you doing?"

"Thanks, Dad, and I'm great," I responded and meant it. "I wanted to invite you guys to dinner Friday. Are you busy?"

The surprised look in their faces was priceless. I needed to try to bridge the gap and this was a great way to start.

"Yes, we are free for you," Mom said with a satisfied look on her face. She knew what I was trying to do.

"Good, try to be at the house by six, okay?" I said.

"Okay," she said. "I'll bring your favorite chocolate cake for dessert."

"Good, I'll get to see my little man," Dad said.

Mom leaned over to me and kissed my cheek. "I am so proud of you."

I didn't respond but I kissed her back.

"I'll see you guys on Friday," I said, turning to walk toward my car. "Oh and Dad," I said, touching his arm, "forgiveness is on the way. You have to know that it is a process." He looked at me and smiled. It was clear that a burden had been lifted.

I walked to the driver's side of my car, entered it and started the ignition. Driving away, I looked in the rearview mirror and I noticed that I was actually smiling.

"Are you coming in?" Justin asked, standing in the doorway.

His question returned me to the present. Just thinking about how much that visit to New Light helped me caused me to smile.

As Justin met me at the door, we turned to watch Mom, Dad and Adam drive away. The dinner was wonderful and I really felt good, better than I had felt in a long time.

As soon as Mom and Dad left, we mentally turned back the time to our newlywed years and ran upstairs to our bedroom and devoured each other. Needless to say, Justin and I made the most of the time alone. We enjoyed each other and talked. He told me to hold on with regard to work. I silently took his advice and more of his lovin'.

It was only 9:30 p.m. when we decided to get out of the bed and take a trip to the store for ice cream.

When we turned the corner to re-enter our development, my cell phone rang.

"Paige, it's Mom. I am at the hospital. I am not hurt." There was a pregnant pause. "But we had a car accident and your Dad and Adam have been hurt."

I heard myself scream.

Chapter 22

We arrived at the hospital faster than I ever did when I visited Mom during her hospital stay. I ran through the automatic doors and was directed to where Adam was. Mom was standing in the corridor wringing her hands and walking back and forth. She saw me and began to walk briskly toward me.

"Mom, where is he?" I asked, looking around.

"They are both in there." She was staring through two big, white double doors. "They are working on both of them in the same area." Mom's words remained steady.

"What happened?" I asked, not feeling as self-assured about the situation as Mom at that moment.

"We were coming back from getting a milkshake from McDonald's and were at the traffic light. A drunk driver hit us from the side." She moved to sit on a chair and began to rub her legs as if they ached. "It was the side that both your father and Adam were on. Your father was hurt worse than Adam."

I sat down next to Mom. She took my hand and she began to pray.

I couldn't hear what she was saying because I couldn't focus. I just wanted to see my baby. All I could think was how scared he probably was. I began to have thoughts of him being stretched out in a coffin. My head was spinning and my heart felt as if it were going to implode. Anxiety, fear and anger wrapped around me like a cocoon.

Just when I thought I was going to scream to stop my mind from spiraling with thoughts of death, I heard a calm voice whisper to my heart.

We are troubled on every side, yet not distressed; we are perplexed, but not in despair.

Recognizing the words from the Word of God, I exhaled and then allowed my mind to clear. Finally being able to focus, I tightened my grip on my mom's hand. Adam's face, with his familiar smile, crossed my mind like a mental motion picture. Mom ended her prayer. I hadn't heard a word. Justin rushed in to meet us. He looked at me strangely.

"Are you okay?" he asked.

"Yes, I am okay. I am just waiting to see Adam."

"Have you talked with the attending physician?" Justin asked, continuing to stare at me with a questioning gaze.

"No. Mom just told me what happened. The doctors are working on both of them in there." I mimicked Mom and pointed in the same direction she did only moments ago.

Justin pulled me to him and spoke softly. "Are you sure that you are okay? I don't understand how you can be so calm right now," he said, looking deeply into my eyes, trying to read me.

"I just know that Adam will be okay. I have to learn to place my trust in Jesus," I said, holding his face in my hands as a tear escaped his right eye and made its way down his cheek. I kissed it, tasting the salt and said, "For our light affliction, which is but for a moment worketh for us a far more exceeding and eternal weight of glory."

"Thank you, Jesus," Justin said and kissed me.

I heard the two large double white doors open and two African-American physicians stepped toward Mom. Justin and I rushed over to where they were, just in time for Justin to catch Mom before she lost her balance.

Dad's injuries were extremely serious and they didn't think that Dad would last through the night. He was semi-conscious. His left arm and leg was broken. His head was essentially sliced by the windshield glass which injured his cranial cavity. There was a great deal of internal bleeding because of the extensive organ damage. They had been able to stop the bleeding but because of his advanced age, they were not confident that he would recover. If he did make it, brain damage would be a certainty. I placed my arms around Mom as the doctor spoke.

"Adam was very lucky. A couple of ribs are broken and there are deep lacerations on his torso, but he will recover," explained the doctor who had introduced himself to us as Dr. Lawson. "You may see Adam but he is not awake."

"We will keep you posted but I think that it is best that you contact the rest of your family in the event that Mr. Hunter expires during the night," Dr. Faison stated. He apologized for providing such a dismal prognosis. He and Dr. Lawson turned and returned the way they had come.

"Mom, you know that Dad has fight in him. You have to be strong for him the way he was strong for you," I said.

"I know that's right," Mom said. She patted my hand and walked toward the doors. "Go and see your son. I am going to see your father. Do not call your sisters until I come back out," she said with a determined voice.

Justin and I went in to see Adam. I walked up to his bedside and just stood there watching him breathe. His perfectly smooth face had been bandaged on the left and his little duck lips were swollen. I didn't dare look at the rest of him for fear of losing my strong resolve not to cry. I knew he was a light sleeper and he'd hear me. Justin gently placed his hand over Adam's. He prayed. After he prayed, we kissed our brown cherub, verbally thanked God for him and his recovery and left the room.

Mom appeared. "There isn't any need to call your sisters. He's gone." Her voice was trembling but her eyes didn't waver. I instantly ran to Mom and held her. She accepted my embrace but there weren't any tears. "He said he needed to go. He said that he could go and meet the Master knowing that he had your forgiveness and the forgiveness of your sisters. He said he was proud of his little princesses and knew that you all would be okay. His only regret was that he would not get to meet his new grandchild." Mom's eyes were glassy. I embraced her and she continued. "I promised to tell the baby all about him."

Mom explained that there wasn't need for a large home-going service. He only wanted his family to have a simple memorial service and that could happen at anytime. He could be buried as soon as arrangements could be made. "I am going to honor his request," she concluded. She started to walked and then paused to looked back toward the large doors and said, "I am just so glad that he was right with God." She closed her eyes. "Thank you for your mercy, Jesus. You are truly faithful."

A persistent tear received a pardon and was freed from her eye. She blinked and the lone tear of joy and loss was released.

"I am spending the night here, so could you go home and get some toiletries and clothes for me?" I asked Justin.

A current of understanding passed between us and he kissed my cheek, hugged my mom and turned to leave.

Many people didn't understand why Dad didn't want a church home-going service. Those who knew Dad understood and that was all that mattered. It was a peaceful memorial service and to my surprise Mom said that Dad wanted me to sing.

"He always loved to hear you sing, Paige," Mom encouraged. I agreed and sang "Precious Lord." It was one of Dad's favorites.

The service was held at their house. Only family and a few choice friends were in attendance. Karlie made the trip with her husband and Tara. It was so good to see her.

"You seem to be holding up well," she said as I walked her out to her car. Tyson was talking with Justin a couple of paces behind.

"I am," I said. "Forgiving is so underrated."

She chuckled. "I am so happy that you and he were able to clear the air before he passed. This was all in the plan, I am sure."

Her eyes searched mine as if she wanted to check the climate before asking a question. I guess I subconsciously gave her the all-clear sign because she stopped walking and turned toward me.

"Paige, has it been made clear to you?" she asked expectantly.

Knowingly, I nodded and said, "Crystal clear." I smiled. "I think that I knew it all the time but refused to allow myself to believe because of so many past disappointments that seemed to have been coupled with His involvement. He had to make himself clear to me and to me only. The influence of church was not a variable. God spoke directly to me and will continue to speak to me. I am so glad that He did not give up me because I sure would have. I may not have wanted to hear him but He is and will always be there."

"You can't run anymore," she stated as a reminder.

"I am one step ahead of you." We resumed our walking and then I said, "I joined Zion House the Sunday after Dad passed. I repented some time ago and asked the Lord for forgiveness and being true to his word, He has forgiven me."

"Praise God!" she yelled. She looked around as if she had dropped something. "Hey, where is Tara?" Karlie asked.

"The last time I saw her, she was the in guest room with Adam, playing checkers," I responded.

"I think that we have a budding mini-romance," Karlie said with a slight smirk. "They are inseparable."

"I know."

"Tyson, go inside and tell her that we have got to go," Karlie said to Tyson as she placed a bag into trunk of her midnight-blue Honda Civic.

Tara, a vision of her father, appeared. Her straight, coal-black hair was secured into two ponytails, one on top of the other. She skipped down the front walk in her velvet blue dress. Her eyes were dark brown and her dimples were displayed as she halted in front of her mom with a grin showing her missing front tooth.

"It's time to go, baby," Karlie said.

"Oh, I wanted to stay and play with Adam a little while longer," she said, her smile slowly turning into a pout.

"I promise we'll be back so that you can spend some more time with Adam," Karlie said.

Tara looked at me for confirmation.

"Yes, Tara. You will be coming back during the Christmas holidays," I promised.

"Really? Thanks, Aunt Paige," she said as she hugged me. "I'll see you then."

She hopped into the car and closed the door. We all exchanged hugs and promised to keep the holidays open.

Later that evening, once all of the extended family was gone and it was just the immediate family, I walked into Mom's room to check on her. She had taken a nap earlier but seemed to be awake when I leaned over her bed.

"Are you okay?" I inquired, noticing that she still looked tired.

"I will be," she said, nodding as she took my hand.

Celia, Darlene and Loni entered the room as if on cue.

"Girls, I know that your dad was not a perfect man but you have got to believe that he loved you. He didn't always know how to show you, but he did. The only love he received was from his mother but that was only when she wasn't too tired to show it."

She moved to sit up and placed her head that was little matted from her slumber on the cushioned headboard.

"I am sure that you could have been disappointed with me for staying with him all those years but it was only because I knew him. You could easily blame me for the hell that you had to endure. There isn't any excuse but I think that through it all, you all have learned what not to do and how not to act. Most importantly, you know what is real and what is not."

"Mom, you don't have to go through all of this. We made our peace with Dad before he left," Loni said, rubbing her belly. "I am just sorry he won't know my baby or the babies that Celia and Darlene will have."

Mom reached out to all of us and we hugged. "That was his one regret," she said. "I am proud of each of you. Learn from the mistakes that I made. Because all of you know Christ, don't let anyone make you doubt Him."

Chapter 23

The weeks seemed to pick up speed as the enrollment season became more hectic. My days were becoming a blur and I found myself becoming tired of fighting with the Rosenfeld account team. In mid-November, open enrollment neared its end and the meetings were almost over. Unfortunately, it was brought to my attention that some of the reps who had agreed to present the information at the meetings for enrollment did not meet the client's standards. Much to my dismay it was the Rosenfeld account meetings.

According to Myra, who stated that she spoke directly with the client, the representatives were not familiar with the product and could not confidently respond to the questions posed by the prospective membership. After hearing this, I was shocked. I had provided the representatives with the finalized presentation, benefit designs, client information. I also provided any communications that I shared with the client to ensure that all were on the same page. I had no doubt that this would be an easy task for the representatives. I even spoke with a couple of them to make certain that they knew the material. They seemed clear and could simply answer any questions that the members may have had about the benefit plan . To hear that four of the ten meetings that required a counterpart representative bombed, resulted in my being more that a little concerned.

In an effort to arrive at an complete understanding as to what occurred at the client meetings and to possibly prevent this embarrassing travesty from happening to another colleague, I scheduled a conference call with Myra, Leann, and June.

Admittedly, the call was quite tense. Myra was unmistakably terse but I was determined not to take the fall for what was clearly not my fault. It was impossible for me to facilitate all of the meetings. I was not anyone's boss so I couldn't train them on how to present but only provide them with the data and information required to aid them.

Prior to the call, I was checking my e-mails because I was scheduled to leave town that afternoon and told all that I would be out of the office and wouldn't have access to e-mail. While on the call and during my explanation of what had occurred and how all the necessary preparations were made for the reps to be successful, an e-mail popped in from Myra.

It said, "This N_____ is full of poop. She sounds so uppity. I can't stand her." As I began to comprehend the words of e-mail, my verbal account of the turn of events became lodged in my throat. I gathered myself quickly, continued and concluded. Myra obviously had no idea that the e-mail transmitted to all of the attendees. Could she be that stupid? Apparently so. Immediately after the call, I called June and told her of the e-mail. She seemed to be shocked and stated that she had not received the communication. I knew that she was on the distribution and received the e-mail. I don't know why I was surprised when she blatantly lied. What threw me for an even bigger loop was that she had the nerve to ask me to remain on the account. She asked me to call her back when I got back in town. I decided that as hard as it was going to be, the only way I was going to win this battle was to remove myself from the matter and let God solve it for me. "Jesus, you have this," I said aloud. *For we wrestle not against flesh and blood, but against principalities, against powers, against the rulers of the darkness of this world, against spiritual wickedness in high places.*

"Thank you, Lord," I said. The words were not a whisper. No longer was the voice still and small. God spoke to me in rush of comfort that left me with a feeling that I was going to be victorious. I admitted to myself that I was concerned about the outcome but I was determined to leave it to God.

Rather than working the day after returning from my business trip, I decided to call in sick. I told myself that I needed a mental day.

I spent my day at Mom's and told her that I no longer had a feeling of emptiness. The void was filled with my relationship with Jesus. I had to admit that I felt stupid because He was there all the time and I just had to stop being so angry, afraid and worst of all, stubborn. Justin and I were more in sync than I could remember. Adam was on the road to recovery and would be back to normal in no time.

On my way home, I stopped at Dad's grave. I talked to God while at the site.

Still unsure as to what I should do about the situation, I returned home. When peeking in my office, I noticed that I had a message on my work phone. Yielding to temptation, I pressed "play."

"Mrs. Covington, this is Ramsey Inbush, of Benefits At Work, Inc. I was afforded the opportunity to meet you in late August. We represented Rosenfeld Data as their consultant. I was very impressed with your presentation. You seemed very well-versed in your company's products and knew how to communicate what the member needed to do to be successful when choosing their health insurance carrier. We have a number of clients that are not as large as Rosenfeld but are in need of your expertise and obvious professionalism. I know that this is quite unorthodox, but there was something about you and we didn't want to miss an opportunity like this." Mr. Inbush paused and then said, "We were hoping that you would be interested in an opportunity to possibly meet with me to discuss a career change…" I let the message continue and ended the recording.

"Jesus, you are the bomb!" I said aloud.

After talking it over with Justin, I returned the call the next day and the opportunity of a lifetime was offered. I scheduled a meeting with Mr. Inbush. He insisted on coming to meet with me at a nearby swanky restaurant. He mentioned during our lunch interview that he was a Christian and that it was placed on his heart to give me a call and to offer me a job. He said that he didn't understand it but a week later one of his top executives decided to leave her position to stay home with her children.

He laughed when he said, "God always know what He is doing, even when we don't."

A couple of weeks later, while discussing another account with Leann, she asked how I was doing since it had been weeks since I discussed the whole Rosenfeld issue. My response to her was simple. "God has it under control."

I didn't want to tell her that I had reported Myra to Human Resources and they had conducted and investigation and had levied charges against her for her conduct. I didn't want her to know the specifics but I knew that she would find out sooner or later. Myra wasn't fired but she was severely reprimanded, the incident was placed in her file and to make matters worse, she was removed from the Rosenfeld account and didn't receive the commission from the influx of enrollees for the HRA account. I knew that was the worst part for her. I also reported June, as she did not act in a manner that was appropriate when it was clear that the comments made were racially motivated. She would get her comeuppance as well.

On the last day before my Christmas vacation, I wrote a letter to both June and her direct report advising them of my resignation effective immediately. The letter was sent as an attachment to an e-mail marked urgent. I noted the reasons for my departure and could not promise that those reasons would not be made public. I was sure that it would be bad publicity for BHN. I really didn't have any intentions on telling anyone but if the subject came up, I was not going to lie.

An hour after the e-mail was sent, my phone began to ring. I decided not to answer it.

Much to my surprise, I didn't feel any pangs of guilt. I had secured the position with Benefits at Work, Inc., and would be starting the Tuesday after Martin Luther King's birthday. The great part of the deal was that I would be able to continue to work from home.

"God you are awesome," I said as I began to just worship Him for my victory.

Chapter 24

Justin and I planned on going to church for New Year's Eve and then going out for a New Year's dinner later that day. Mom said that she would stay at our house and watch Adam just in case we wanted to go out for dessert after service. The Christmas holiday was difficult but we made certain that Mom was surrounded with family, good memories and lots of laughter.

Feelings of sadness did manage to creep in when we all gathered at the Christmas table. Dad was not sitting at the head. Blue was given the task of carving the turkey. That was an occupation that Dad proudly performed. In honor of him only, we prayed as he would have. Tyler prayed a prayer just like Dad. It didn't seem to bother me that we were standing around the table for almost twenty minutes. I think we were grateful for the memories.

"I hope you heard that," Tyler said as Loni nudged him while rubbing her belly.

"As long as your prayer was, I am sure that he did," Mom said, chuckling.

We ate and laughed and even sang together. It was so nice to really feel like a family. We weren't putting on airs and there wasn't a need to.

As I turned off the shower and tuned out the memory of Christmas day, I opened the bathroom door.

Justin was sitting on the bed putting on his socks. I watched him for a moment and then walked over to give him a hug. I had just toweled off and the aroma of pink grapefruit was in the air.

"Hmmm. You smell good," he said as he kissed my ear. "Do we have time for a quick…?"

"Thanks and no, but I'll be sure to let you ring in the New Year correctly when we get back."

I could hear him exhale and I laughed aloud.

"I should be ready in twenty minutes," I told him as I walked in the closet and pulled out my black dress.

"Good, your mom is downstairs."

"Is she here already?" I asked, surprised. I took a quick look at the digital clock on my night stand and realized that I had better get moving. It was already 9:00 p.m. Services were scheduled to start at 10:00 p.m.

Justin was completely dressed when he announced that he would go downstairs and see how Mom and Adam were making out. I promised Adam that he could stay up for one hour after we left and not a minute longer.

Slipping on my patent leather sling backs and fastening my earrings, I made my way down the stairs. Both of my men whistled as I descended. I could feel my face becoming warm. I loved the attention from my men. The black dress was simple but it definitely accentuated my curves. My hair was down and bumped at the ends.

As we entered the family room, I heard the phone ring. Justin rose to get it while I gave Mom some last minute instructions on the house alarm, where we kept Adam's medicines and the like.

Justin came rushing into the room and exclaimed, "Loni is labor!"

I turned to Mom. "Isn't she about a month early?" I asked with a confused expression.

"No, I'd say she is right on time," Mom said with a wink.

"Let me go change my clothes so that we can get to the hospital," I said as I took off my shoes to head upstairs.

Justin grabbed my hand. "No time, baby. Tyler said she was nine centimeters dilated and one hundred percent effaced."

I knew what that meant and put on my shoes and grabbed my wrap from the closet.

"You two go and keep me posted. I'll stay here with Adam. Tell Loni that I am with her," Mom said as she grinned. "Now get going."

As I buckled my seat belt, I leaned over to Justin and said, "It's about time we are going to the hospital for some good news."

Ivana Hunter Lyons was born about an hour after we arrived. She was nine pounds and eight ounces. It seemed that Loni was further along than she even thought when she initially announced her pregnancy. The baby was full-term and was a beautiful chocolate doll. She looked a lot like Dad around the eyes and she had those Hunter lips. The sharp contrast between her light eyes and her dark complexion made her appear exotic. Tyler was going to have to watch her when she became a teenager.

Loni didn't seem as tired as I felt after I gave birth to Adam. She was talkative and laughed a bit. The episiotomy was a necessary evil because of Ivana's size but she said she would have endured anything to bring this baby into the world.

As I watched Tyler and Loni smiling while I held the new addition to our family, I thought of how proud Dad would have been. He had another princess. For an instant I thought I smelled his cologne. I just realized that I had really forgiven Dad and wanted him to be here with us to witness the dawning of a new generation. As I sang to my beautiful niece, I thought about how God's word was so true. Because when I tried not worry about anything and sought the kingdom, all of my wants and needs had been provided, even the ability to forgive. Acknowledging the voice of God as my inner witness and welcoming it, freed me to trust again. God was truly an Awesome Wonder, I thought.

I was truly beginning to enjoy every aspect of my life. My love for my husband had bloomed unfettered like a spring flower. The walls of that Jericho were tumbling down. I was singing again and had joined the Zion House Choir. The nervousness when praising God for fear of who was watching or judging me was gone and my voice had an anointing like never before. I looked forward to what God had in store for me and my family. I was truly renewed.

Although I missed Dad and bad memories crept into my mind from time to time, I knew that he was with us and toward the end he proved that he wasn't the same man. More importantly, God was with me and the Holy Spirit was my guide. I had come to recognize His importance and never wanted to be without Him. I truly believed that I could do all things through Jesus Christ who continued to strengthen me.

There wasn't anything fake or phony about that.

The End!